THE KITABIAN DIMENSION

SANDEEP K. AGGARWAL

iUNIVERSE, INC.
NEW YORK   BLOOMINGTON

The Kitabian Dimension

iUniverse books may be ordered through booksellers or by contacting:

iUniverse
1663 Liberty Drive
Bloomington, IN 47403
www.iuniverse.com
1-800-Authors (1-800-288-4677)

ISBN: 978-1-4401-7443-8 (sc)
ISBN: 978-1-4401-7445-2 (dj)
ISBN: 978-1-4401-7444-5 (ebk)

Printed in the United States of America

iUniverse rev. date: 10/28/2009

PROLOGUE

Two thousand years ago, when an Australian naval team was returning from a mission in the South Pacific, they drifted off course due to inclement weather.

The crew spotted a chain of islands, and the captain decided to drop anchor rather than continue with the journey. The crew questioned the captain's motives, but was told that any treasures found would be shared. The captain dispatched a recon team to scout out the terrain. The leader of the team selected three of his top warriors and paddled a small rowboat to shore. They carried swords for protection. "We have to be careful," the leader said as he slowly surveyed the beachhead. When they landed, the team quickly stowed the craft in the brush and charted a course. The leader told two of his warriors to follow a small opening on one side of the beach. He and the remaining warrior found a path on a small ridge leading away from the beach. "Let's go," said the leader. The two groups separated and after about half an hour of negotiating the deep brush, met up at the edge of a lake. Along the way, there was no evidence of human life; just small animals and birds.

"This looks like a peaceful island. Look, there are volcanic mountains in the distance with a river that seems to run into this lake," said one of the team members.

"Let's explore some more," said the leader as he led the entire team a short distance around the lake. From a small gap in the woods across the lake they could see some primitive dwellings. They hid in the underbrush and were able to make out human life. They then made their way back to the beach, located their craft, and sailed back to the ship. They reported back later that night to the captain, carefully detailing their observations.

Though there was evidence of human life, the captain claimed this land as his and named it Wellen, after his son who died heroically in battle.

"What about the natives, sir?" said the leader of the recon team.

"We'll deal with them later," said the captain.

With no treasures in hand, the crew sailed back to Australia. When the chain of islands they had found were mapped out by the Australian cartographers, they resembled a dolphin. The Australians named this island chain the Kirio archipelago.

The captain told his colleagues of the discovery and insisted that he get the credit and be allowed to run the island chain. The Australian government and other island nations let the local island leaders live in peace. The captain was relegated to the western Australian naval fleet.

The name Wellen remained, and over the next fifty years travelers from other countries began to populate the area. One traveler, a pioneer in mountain climbing, was quite amazed by the size of the island. He estimated that the diameter was at least fifty miles. The mountain range, which encircled one half of the island, rendered access by sea impossible. Air travel was restricted to those daring enough to pilot a hot air balloon, but as the volcanic mountain range was rather treacherous, no one attempted this approach. The original inhabitants of Wellen never witnessed any life or activity on the other half of the island, which they named the Kitab.

At about the same time Wellen was founded, Australia's national security office set up an independent council to patrol the activity of the island nations surrounding Wellen. This council was distinct from the larger South Pacific security group. They recruited warriors from neighboring islands and around the world. As the mountain range was a mystery, the Australians constructed a defense system in the event that a warring civilization existed on the other side of the mountains. They wanted to maintain harmony among the other island nations in the Kirio archipelago. Representatives from all the island nations in the South Pacific and the main continents incorporated this small council. This served as a form of checks and balances. Wellen was by far the most advanced in this string of island nations, and in a fifty-year span grew as a metropolis that could have rivaled any city on the mainland. Australia left governance up to the Wellenites. The inhabitants held elections every two years to select a mayor. In the beginning, most of the candidates were ruthless and ran the island like a dictatorship. At the next election, however, the people were more careful in their selection and found a benevolent leader who maintained a democracy. The natives were afraid of the previous leaders and kept to themselves. They lived in the bush on the southeastern half of the island. The mayor was educated in Australia and had an open mind. He approached the natives and involved them in the politics of the island as part of mutual respect. That was how he discovered that the natives resolved their differences through a game called Retsel.

Retsel consisted of a three-dimensional board. The middle level contained a row of five circles separated by spaces at one end of the board. The next row consisted of four squares with one large circle in the middle of the row with two of the squares on either side. The next row also had five circles separated by spaces. The same configuration was on the other side and represented the opponent. There was a large space of alternating squares and circles separating the two configurations and on each of the two other levels. There were a total of thirty pieces, fifteen for each player, aligned on the lowest level only. Ten were the same size, resembling pyramids made of pewter, four were chrome and shaped like cylinders, and one, the most important, was gold, resembling a crown. The pyramids were arranged on the circles, with the cylinders on the row of squares. The crown was placed on the single circle. Play commenced with movement of any piece as long as it remained on its designated shape. The pyramids could move in any direction, including over another piece, but only as far as the next circle. The cylinders could only slide to the next square along any dimension, whereas the crown could only move laterally or vertically along the squares, again one at a time. One could capture the opponent's piece in any dimension. The object was to capture the crown but only in another dimension than the original and in the time allotted. Points were awarded for how quickly players captured their opponent's pieces and the total number of pieces captured.

Over the course of thirteen hundred years, Wellen flourished as more and more travelers populated the island. Once air travel became possible, aerial photographs were taken of the island. In the valley below the Kitabian Mountains, there was indeed a civilization that appeared rather simple in design. On one occasion, a pilot had flown too close and crashed in the Kitab. The leaders let him go with the caveat that no one ever fly over their airspace or interfere with them again. The pilot did not have a chance to learn much of the region as he was quickly jailed after his crash landing and kept in prison until his release. The Kitab remained a mystery to everyone as its inhabitants stayed isolated and did not allow free communication.

In time, selected government officials were permitted to speak with the leaders to assure that peace was their main agenda. The borders were eventually loosened in the narrowest sense. There was very strict security in the event that Wellenites or others wished to visit. All information gathered was confiscated at the border. Tourists were only permitted to enter selected areas. As a result, information was scarce. The founding papers and charter were also kept heavily guarded. The actual details of the origins of the Kitab were not clearly known.

Wellen was a peaceful society and for the most part safe. Life was simple. Though there was the usual affluent minority, they weren't flagrant. There was plenty of industry, including a large service sector. The people were friendly. Most of the inhabitants lived modestly. The island was fifty miles wide and twenty-five miles long, split evenly between the two halves. The Kitabian Mountains served as the dividing line.

In the latter half of the eighteenth century, Wellen formed two universities on the island that became world famous, not only in general studies but also in nontraditional medicine and tropical studies. In keeping with Wellen's philosophy of an all-inclusive government, the mayor at the time invited the tribal chief to become an adjunct professor in herbal and nontraditional medicine at the medical school. The mayor also brought Retsel, which had continued to be passed down from one generation to the next, to Wellen. The game was soon incorporated into the fabric of everyday life. The chief had taught the university chess teams some of the more intricate strategies of the game.

The intellectual community in Wellen, not unlike others, was made up of prima donnas who needed to exert their raison d'être. The two universities, Sci Tech and Libertarian, were separated by the river on the outskirts of the city center. They kept their philosophies consistent. Though students could choose either university, most based their decision upon the philosophy of one over the other. Typically, science and math prevailed at Sci Tech University whereas philosophy and English predominated at the Libertarian University. Graduate schools existed at both, although the differences were less at that level. The medical school was shared between the two universities.

During the founding of the universities, a group of students from Sci Tech formed an underground organization that set as its main purpose control of their university over the other for fear of extinction. They reasoned that the other university would prosper, because they promoted open expression. They felt that this would dissuade students from entering their own institution, ultimately leading to anarchy and loss of control. They called themselves the Directors. They preferred the prevailing dogma and did not want eccentric and eclectic ideas pervading the culture. In general, the members were leaders in society, made up of entrepreneurs, lawyers, and philanthropists of the university. They were for the most part quiet and would support the university through volunteer efforts and donations. They never disclosed the name of their organization for fear of repercussions to their families. The central government was neutral and let the universities promote individual thought as this served as a balance.

At the turn of the present century, Sci Tech University serendipitously discovered an ancient civilization buried deep in the dense vegetation. They thought this was the link to the Kitab, because the discovery was located at the foothills of the Kitabian Mountains. As relations between the two universities had become strained, the scientists at Sci Tech did not share this information with Libertarian University. There was so much complaining that Wellen decided to close one of the two universities. The government stopped all funding and forbade any further excavation of the site. Foreign concerns were also discouraged and in fact banned to fund exploration. They also withheld this information from the Kitabian government.

Despite the fact that Sci Tech discovered this civilization, the Directors feared that their alma mater would be chosen as the one to close. They tended to be too dogmatic and reluctant to move toward the center.

One university group had wanted to build a scientific program at the exclusion of another group at the rival program. Other disciplines followed suit and eventually everyone was fighting and backstabbing each other. As there was no amicable solution, political and social concerns finally came to a head. The university leaders were not able to present a unified front to obtain funding and soon began to lose credibility around the world. The prominent business leaders in Wellen felt that the pulse of the city was becoming less palpable. The chancellors of the universities, in conjunction with the Wellen chamber of commerce, decided to settle this dispute with a Retsel match, as they had done on many occasions in the past, generation after generation.

CHAPTER I

The great hall was crowded, the air filled with cigarette smoke and sweat. Winter in Wellen was usually blistering hot. The month was January and lived up to its reputation. The last time it rained was two weeks ago. The beaches were full of people trying to cool off. One man took his chair into the lake and sat there till sunset.

The faint rumble of voices in the background punctuated an eerie silence that added to the tension. The fate of two academic institutions depended upon the performance of the master strategist, known as Chaych. He was on staff at the Libertarian University. A brilliant Retsel player, rather reserved, he had a thin build. He wore rectangular shaped, black, tortoise shelled glasses and a weathered blue blazer with gray slacks. His long, shoulder length, jet black hair was always in disarray. As a toddler, he had the uncanny ability to anticipate ahead of time two or three of his opponents' moves and then in three dimensions. His challenger today, Dr. N. B. Korbin, was a formidable adversary who was a legend in his youth. Now approaching seventy, he was of stocky build with ruddy cheeks and had a sanguine personality to match. He could, however, beat anyone half his age with a degree of finesse hardly seen by his contemporaries.

Offstage, prior to the start of the match, the two were seated in a bare room. Korbin was deep in thought, almost unaware that Chaych was seated across from him. He was staring at the yellow walls, stained from many years of cigarette smoke. There were no wall hangings. Sweat beaded on his forehead, glistening in the pale light. The chair beneath him creaked. Just as a stream was about to roll down Korbin's well-lined face, Chaych stood up slowly, placed his hand on the old, dusty card table and asked, "Are you okay?"

"Yes, I am just meditating, as I customarily do prior to any match," said Korbin.

Chaych sat back down and suddenly blurted, "You know, we're only pawns ourselves today." He had a habit of saying whatever came to his mind without first censoring his thoughts. Noticing Korbin's puzzled look, Chaych was exasperated. He went on to explain. "The result of today's match will determine which academic center gains control over the other. This would in effect lead to a merger, creating a unified institution. For some, this would mean the end of free expression and critical thinking as in most monopolies." Chaych stood up and raised his clenched fist into the air and said, "I can hear it now; down with the rhetoric and let dogma prevail!"

The veins in Chaych's scalp began to pound, with one curiously coursing through his temple as he started to bang loudly on the card table. Saliva pooled at the corners of his mouth. Korbin was sitting erect in his chair, amazed at the sight in front of his eyes. He began to frown and protruded his lips. He worried that Chaych would inflict harm. Korbin stood up and walked toward the door, then quickly turned around and said in a quiet voice, "Calm down."

After awhile, Chaych regained his composure. One of the security guards posted outside of their room came in to check on them. "Everything okay in here?" he asked. "I thought someone was dying."

"We're all right," said the pair in unison.

"We were just having a healthy debate," said Korbin.

When the guard left, Korbin resumed his meditation, and Chaych thought about the future. Suddenly, Chaych got up again, but this time walked toward the door. He felt it was his duty to explain his philosophy over the university battle. He listened for activity outside. When he was convinced all was quiet, he said, "Personally, I don't care and am not interested in these political maneuvers. The administration usually doesn't change much, unless the government slashes budgets and grants."

Korbin thought about this for a few minutes and was half surprised but also did not appear to be concerned. He was somewhat startled by the outburst, but this time Chaych didn't strike out physically, so he felt somewhat more at ease. After a few minutes, he looked up, saw that Chaych was quietly sitting in his chair, and said, "I also don't take much stock in these political games, but I do have more interest from an academic standpoint as I prefer the philosophy of my institution more. Yours is more liberal and requires more emphasis on alternative or eclectic thought that for an old man like me is rather extreme." By now, Korbin was speaking a bit louder, with sweat running down his forehead. Chaych had never seen him so passionate. Korbin continued, "Granted, I'm old, but I still function, and I work as much as someone younger." He stood up and walked around the room, then looked down at Chaych with his experienced, professorial eyes and said, "I'm still active at my university, teaching and writing strategy. Whatever the outcome, our match will be quite instructive today." Chaych looked up at Korbin sheepishly while he stood silently for a few seconds. Finally, Korbin sat down, smiled, and said collegially, "I look forward to playing against someone so young and prodigal as you."

"For me, this will be a crowning achievement in my career also, to play someone as accomplished as you, a true master. It is rather odd that we have never played," said Chaych, leaning forward with his elbows resting on the table.

"I agree," said Korbin, raising his eyebrows and placing his fingers on his chin and lower lip. He went to say, "This is part of the problem. We have all become so insular in our own universities that sharing information is taboo. For many years there was a healthy rivalry. When research projects funded by one university would have truly benefited society, this was shared with the other and promoted as a joint venture. Over time, however, secrecy and insecurity prevailed. Some of my colleagues were deluded into thinking that if the details of a project were known, the university would lose funding and its reputation. As such, ideas were no longer shared and collaboration came to a halt."

Chaych stood up and started pacing the floor. "This egregious behavior means that one of the universities has to close or simply merge with the other to avoid further conflict."

Korbin replied with a disgusted look on his face, "I know. In fact, livelihoods are now at stake, as downsizing will surely occur. This is especially alarming for the junior faculty. I overheard a young man in the economics lab lamenting that the lab would close. There are similar worries throughout the system. All we can do at this point is wait. Senior faculty are making sure that their projects are up and running and sound to prevent shutdown. It is sad that we had to meet up this way, so late in our careers. Anyway, what is done is done. I have read your books on strategy and now can't wait to see them implemented."

The bell sounded, signaling the two players to enter the great hall. They walked with their hands gracefully at their sides and heads bowed in reverence to the moment. The Retsel table was on a stage under bright lights. They were escorted by security guards. No one spoke. The hall was quiet with an overbearing sense of anticipation. The players arrived with conspicuous humility and took their seats. There was a large-screen TV behind them, displaying the Retsel board for those in the back and outside. Those who belonged to Chaych's university sat on his side of the hall and Korbin's supporters on the other side. The front rows were reserved for faculty. As customary for Retsel matches, the faculty wore official university uniforms of gray slacks and navy blue blazers with their university emblem sewn on the breast pocket. The seats were worn from use but still comfortable. Students were in the rear and were excused from wearing formal attire. The middle rows were for dignitaries, politicians, businessmen, and one Jim Maklober, the chief detective who belonged to the elite security unit. He was somewhat stocky, average height, with a rather rumpled appearance but clean shaven. Maklober had been a wrestler in high school, and he still kept in shape and was quite strong. He had a full head of hair, but his eyes had started to show some of the strain of his job. He was answerable to both heads of the institutions and also to the South Pacific Security Council (SPSC), which by now commanded quite a presence in the world of politics. In fact, they were instrumental in organizing a central communication center to monitor the activities of high profile criminals.

Maklober knew of the importance of the match and was present as both bodyguard and riot control. Some members of the audience also consisted of special interest groups, including Maklober's girlfriend, Yarmin, who led a small liberal watchdog group. She was an attractive, small-boned brunette whose size didn't stop her from being an influential activist. Maklober had known her from previous events and was impressed by her fortitude and charm. They had gone out on several occasions. They usually met in small cafeteria-like dining establishments near closing time due to the constraints of their jobs. Talk was usually lively and centered on political and social concerns, as Yarmin was always promoting some cause. Maklober mostly listened.

His work, though interesting, would never impassion someone to the extent of worthy or even controversial discussion.

As Maklober sat next to Yarmin, awaiting the start of the Retsel match, he drifted off into deep thought, recalling their date about a week ago. It was ten o'clock and they were listening to some music at the neighborhood pub. He liked his beer, and it showed. Earlier that evening he had just finished up on a long case. The perpetrator was rather elusive and enigmatic. Maklober found his quarry in cyberspace and arrested him. At the pub, Yarmin asked about the case. After Maklober described the circumstances, Yarmin asked, "You mean, Moke?"

"Yeah, but his name is Moch, rhymes with coach. Have you heard of him?" asked Maklober.

"Yeah, there was some talk about him in our organization, but nobody knew the details."

"No one does, unfortunately," said Maklober. "All we do know is that he always manages to round up a good team of lawyers. He'll probably get off on a technicality once again."

"That's terrible," said Yarmin.

"I know, but we're hoping the prosecutor can make it stick. We believe we have all the details straight."

"Even with that, I'm sad to say, our legal system rewards showmanship," said Yarmin.

The buzzer in the great hall rang out, signaling the start of the match and startling Maklober out of his recollections. He was immediately on high alert, scanning the entire room and upper balconies. His phone started ringing. As he surveyed the TV screen, the Retsel match, and the audience, he answered calls and dispatched his plainclothes security guards to various posts in the great hall. This way he knew exactly what was going on at all times. From time to time he ventured outside, where there were protesters of this match and special interest groups. Uniformed policeman were stationed for riot control. A large TV screen was mounted on the building with the local broadcast station providing the play-by-play.

The match began without fanfare. The players were entirely enthralled by the magnitude of the match, not so much for political reasons but rather academic. Korbin's opening moves were unlike any Chaych had seen before. Korbin had methodically and like clockwork set up the board elegantly to capture the crown. There were occasional murmurs from the audience, but for the most part there was complete silence. After Chaych's next move, Korbin broke out into a sweat and sat in silence pondering his options. He knew time was running out. Korbin glanced at his opponent, seeing nothing in his expression. After much deliberation, Korbin slowly advanced his hand to make his next move.

Chaych could see a subtle and momentary tremor in Korbin's outstretched finger as he let go of the piece and rested his hand back on the table. Chaych now sat back, his head looking down at the board, trying to maintain as much of a poker face as he could muster. Then, ever so slightly, he raised his eyebrows in enlightenment and realized that by viewing the board in another dimension and calculating two steps ahead, Korbin had actually exposed his crown in such a way that Chaych could now capture it. It was so simple, yet Chaych pondered and wondered if this were simply a trap.

Experienced Retsel players in the audience did not see this flaw and silently watched in awe. After careful evaluation, Chaych moved one of his pyramids into position and withdrew his hand slowly, resting it on the table. He had to await Korbin's next move and hoped for the expected gap to open. His face was completely still. There was no hint of deception.

After Korbin's move, this was indeed the case. Chaych was about to make his move, but suddenly he froze. He sat staring at the board as if he had never seen it. Murmurs could be heard from the audience. Someone yelled out, "The match is fixed!" A fight was about to break out between the two halves of the audience. The security guards quickly moved in to subdue them. There were more pressing matters at hand now.

"What's wrong?" said the judges.

Chaych could only answer, "I don't know."

He thought about this dilemma as the clock ticked away, but sat in disbelief, perplexed. The judges were about to proclaim Korbin the victor, as the time was almost up.

Suddenly, the noise of the arena increased as members of the community who were watching the match outside saw what happened and rushed into the hallway. The policeman ran in after them and outflanked them. The security guards and police formed a circle around the players. As Maklober was patrolling the hall from a point in the back of the room, he could not see past the circle of guards. One of the security guards who was closest to the table radioed Maklober and told him what was happening with Chaych. Maklober got the message and could not understand the dilemma. He raced to the table, examining the players. He didn't have time to address the audience. He was only focused on the players. Chaych looked at Maklober quizzically and seemed to be dumbfounded, as if he were at a loss to explain himself. Korbin appeared puzzled at Chaych's reaction, and then looked at the board. Even Maklober could see he had exposed his crown. Korbin looked up at Chaych again, blinking his eyes in bewilderment, sweat now streaming down his ruddy cheeks. He awaited Chaych's move. Chaych just sat there.

"I don't want to win by default," Korbin said. He too had waited a long time for this match. As Chaych did not respond, Korbin made eye contact with Maklober and cried out, "Call a doctor!" Maklober had already radioed for an ambulance. Korbin then went over to the judges' table, which was also shielded in the same circle by the police, and said, "You have to stop the clock. This is an extenuating circumstance."

The head judge of the tribunal replied, "Sorry, sir, but the rules state that under no circumstances is the clock to be stopped. The only way is if one player forfeits."

Korbin pounded his fist on the table and glared at the judge in disbelief. He shouted with all his might, "He's having a stroke for God's sake!" With this pronouncement, Chaych's followers screamed in protest and tried to break down the human shield around the players. Maklober quickly mobilized the police units and remaining security squads to contain the crowds. The paramedics were en route. By now, there was a near frenzy outside.

"No one is to enter or leave the building!" Maklober yelled.

Meanwhile, there was a serious situation developing on the other side of the island. Korbin's followers were just about to proclaim victory, when simultaneously there was an emergency announcement broadcast on the big-screen TVs. The Wellenites were in utter amazement as they read the headline, speculating that there was something in common with both situations.

THE KITABIAN GOVERNMENT HAS BEEN PARALYZED

CHAPTER 2

One month prior to the Retsel match, Dr. L. W. Gehirn, "Lewy" as he preferred to be called, a professor of neuropathology at an independent institute that catered to both academic centers, was preparing a prosection of the human brain, revealing the midbrain. He was targeting the substantia nigra, which is involved in Parkinson's disease. He always considered himself fortunate that he wasn't employed by either of the universities. He was able to maintain autonomy this way.

He was startled to hear someone rapidly knocking at his door. The lab was quiet; the students and staff had left long ago. Lewy walked over and opened the door to find a small, thin, gray-haired man smelling of smoke holding some papers in one hand and a worn briefcase in the other. The hand holding his papers shook. "I have to talk with you," he said while looking over his shoulder.

Lewy reluctantly invited him in and asked him to sit down as he walked over to cover the specimen. They sat on stools. The man was rather slight, with stained yellow fingers and a thick voice. His eyelid periodically twitched as he spoke. He had a pencil thin mustache and short, cropped gray hair. He was about to light up a cigarette but was warned not to smoke given all the chemicals nearby.

"I don't have much time; besides this place gives me the creeps," he said.

"Don't worry," said Lewy. "You're safe."

The man sighed, and then said, "I have been asked by my bosses to commission you for a project of utmost secrecy."

"What are you talking about?" asked Lewy.

"It's of no particular significance as to the details of its use," the man said with an air of importance. "Rather, we need a device designed and created to use as we wish," said the man.

"I don't understand. And what if I refuse?" asked Lewy.

"A detailed proposal will be delivered to you in the morning by special courier. Please read it carefully before rendering a decision. This may have economic as well as political fallout. If you do not comply, well, let's just say that your career may suffer at the very least. Also, don't get any bright ideas like calling the authorities."

Lewy was perplexed. He was well-known and had lectured at will at both major universities. He wondered why such a vulgar little man was treating him in this fashion. The man left in a hurry and cautioned once again, "Read the material carefully before you make any rash decisions!"

The package arrived the next morning during the middle of a tutorial session. Lewy was reluctant to open it and did not want to know what it contained. Once he got a break, he left the lab and opened the envelope in the privacy of his office. There was a set of instructions and an illustration, almost like a blueprint.

The instructions read, "We, the Directors, hereby commission you to design a vehicle similar to the enclosed illustration and then help the pilot navigate through the various mountains and valleys of the Kitab. As you know, this is a region inhabited by a people who share uniform thought and work toward a common purpose, which is to survive and produce for the good of the whole. The Superiors oversee the assembly and guide production and transport. They all live in similar dwellings with clean, pristine highways that connect to various regions. Each region produces a particular commodity that is required for the entire area to prosper. There are rivers that traverse the region, scavengers that clean the waterways and streets, and a security force to protect the Kitab from intruders. Visitors are only allowed at certain designated borders and then with written permission obtained prior to their visit."

After Lewy read the instructions and studied the blueprint, he recalled his days in the Kitab years ago when he spent two weeks studying infectious diseases endemic to the area. They rounded with the physicians at the local hospital and were permitted to examine the patients.

Lewy remembered the landscape he saw from the plane's windows. All the homes were uniform in design and lined by white, pristine streets which he likened to gray cells and white matter, or axons, in the brain.

Before his trip, Lewy conducted his own research into the geography and cultural makeup at his local library, which was rather scarce in terms of literature. Once he arrived in the Kitab he found only sketchy maps of the area and little archival information, mostly thoughts as captured by local townspeople from time to time. No one actually kept a diary or account of events over the decades and centuries. Lewy had to rely on word of mouth, which was also rather scant as the people feared repercussions by the Superiors. Over the weekend, he visited the separate regions of the Kitab under the careful scrutiny of the Mahlpatrol, an elite security force.

Lewy later remembered that in a clearing in the deep woods there was a nondescript stone building that housed a factory, affectionately called the "Tangle" by the Kitabians. The workers in this particular factory produced hardware and software components that allowed the Superiors to run their government; specifically, to anticipate changes in the economy and then to devise a solution. They also produced parts to replace defective infrastructure. They created a special relationship with Australia to import steel; otherwise all other materials were available in the area. This in effect represented the executive control center of the Kitab. As one could imagine, this factory, the most crucial one in the entire region, was heavily guarded by the Mahlpatrol. Lewy had learned from some of his colleagues that unbeknownst to the Kitabians and even most of the employees, the senior-most workers would typically complete the final piece of the entire program needed to run the government for the upcoming fiscal year. They were the most trusted of all the employees and rewarded quite well. This was the most updated and advanced segment, known to all as the "Transcript." The information was stored on a twelve-inch disk, housed in a portable, collapsible, plastic case and secured by two small locks requiring separate keys, to which only the Superiors had access.

When Lewy returned home he wrote down his observations, eventually donating them to the local library. He always wanted to return to the Kitab. He liked thinking about his newly-formed colleagues.

A noise in the lab quickly snapped him out of his thoughts. He was still holding the papers sent by the Directors. He got up and placed the papers in his drawer and returned to finish the tutorial session.

A few days later, after Lewy started work on his design for the vehicle as requested by the Directors, he found himself in a dilemma. *How am I going to build this aircraft?* he thought to himself. After careful consideration, he enlisted the services of an aerospace engineer and mathematician he knew from college. They met in a coffeehouse to discuss the particulars, but Lewy was uncomfortable knowing the danger he could put them in. "I know this is a dangerous assignment," he told them. "If I don't comply, I fear for the future of our scientific community."

"This is a huge and risky project, Lewy. What are their intentions?" asked the engineer.

"At this point, I don't know, but anytime anyone wants to go to the Kitab in such a clandestine way, there's bound to be trouble. I can only speculate that they want to steal something of vital importance. This will place Wellen and the Security Council in an awkward position."

Lewy could see the concern and hesitation on their faces.

"Once again, gentleman, I reiterate that this is a dangerous task and that your lives are at stake. What I can assure you, though, is that your names will not be mentioned. I will be the principal on this project."

"How can we do this ethically?" asked the mathematician. "We will be building a weapon, in essence."

"I know, but if we keep it in perspective, we're justified," said Lewy.

"We'll have to think this over, Lewy," said the mathematician. The engineer agreed.

"I understand, but time is of the essence. We have to move quickly on this project. I just don't trust these people," said Lewy.

"Okay, we'll sleep on it and let you know in the morning," said the engineer.

"Please don't let anyone else know about this," said Lewy. The three parted, knowing that this would be a rough night. Lewy went home begrudgingly. He had no one in his life to share this news and didn't want to endanger his other colleagues by making them privy to this knowledge. He thought over the options and after awhile tired himself out enough to fall asleep. He awoke several times in a cold sweat, thinking about his predicament. Morning finally arrived. He took a cold shower and drank some coffee. Lewy went to the lab feeling somewhat refreshed. When he arrived, his two friends were waiting. They were sitting on a bench outside his lab in quiet contemplation. It was Saturday morning and his assistants had not yet arrived. To ensure secrecy, he didn't let anyone know about this project. There was a room adjacent to his office that he made into a small studio apartment in the event that he had to stay late at work, and he took his friends here to discuss their decision.

"So, gentleman, what have you decided?" asked Lewy.

"On behalf of my esteemed colleague, we'll help you, Lewy," said the engineer. Lewy could see small beads of sweat forming on their foreheads and dark circles under their eyes as the engineer spoke.

"I applaud your decision and am eternally grateful," said Lewy.

Work began that same morning. Though the lab would soon be buzzing with activity, Lewy left strict instructions to ensure the scientists' privacy while they worked. Taking his colleagues into the makeshift studio apartment, Lewy guided them in designing a vehicle that could traverse the Kitab. First, they reviewed sketches of the landscape, then the distances involved. After several meetings, the trio not only drafted the blueprints but also built a small model. Once satisfied, the Directors commissioned a crew to build the aircraft. They used parts from old aircrafts. Lewy and his partners were excluded from this phase of the project.

The builders were in awe over the design. The craft was shaped like a leaf of a maple tree, enclosing a small cockpit. On the surface were small particles of debris that resembled branches. A small jet was housed in the rear. The exhaust would have surely attracted attention but was designed in such a way as to simulate that of an ordinary vehicle through an elaborate filtering system. The surface debris would escape radar detection, as this would appear to be a car or truck. In effect the aircraft would blend into the atmosphere of the Kitab as a natural entity. The cockpit contained controls of a rather simple nature only to ensure flight without weaponry; if grounded, it would self-destruct. The pilot could easily sit within the confines of the cockpit and fly the craft. Neither two-way communication nor radar was permitted, as this would be detected. The pilot was to simply fly into the Kitab and navigate through the terrain with maps that he had committed to memory. Once at the site of the factory, he was to fly into the large warehouse and steal the item of interest, using laser technology, which was also set to self-destruct if the plane was grounded.

A few days after Lewy and his partners submitted the design, he heard the familiar rapid knock on his lab door. The little gray-haired man who smelled of smoke had come to visit. Lewy wearily went to the door and let him in.

"How can I help you?" he asked.

"I have a message from the Directors," he said in his own peculiar way. "They congratulate you on your design. Brilliant is the word they used," said the man.

"That's it?" asked Lewy.

"There is nothing else you need to know," said the man. He stood up and pointed his cigarette-stained, trembling index finger at Lewy and said, "Your reward is your lives. No harm will come to you or your families if you keep your silence."

Lewy walked back into the lab and grabbed the door, shouting, "If you're done, get out!"

The man turned around and left. As he was about to enter the hallway, he lit a cigarette and said, "Mark my words!"

Lewy slammed the door shut with a loud bang. He then called his friends to thank them. He didn't share the vulgar details, just telling them that the Directors were satisfied with their design. He knew that their relationship would never be the same again.

Lewy went back to work but was clearly irritated.

***

Moch was on his second martini and smoking a cigar when the Directors entered the room. For major decisions, all five members of the organization had to be present. Moch had been liberated a day prior to the Retsel match. He was taken to one of the director's private offices and cleaned up. The group met him afterwards and discussed the future. The president of the group, Thomas, spoke on behalf of the others. "We can't divulge the reason for this mission, but you will be amply rewarded," he said.

"What do you mean?" asked Moch.

"Let's just say that you won't have to worry about where your next paycheck is coming from, ever again. We will set you up with a monthly allowance that will be held in a trust, controlled by us."

"What if I refuse?" asked Moch.

"We'll send you back to jail and help in any way with the prosecution," said Thomas.

"How do I know I can trust you?" asked Moch.

"You can't. You only have our word."

"I guess I have no choice."

"As a goodwill gesture, we will deposit ten thousand dollars in your checking account tomorrow morning. You can check with your bank before your flight," said Thomas.

"Don't worry, I will."

By the next day, Moch was outfitted and checking out the controls in the cockpit. He memorized his flight plans and mission the night before. He then flew a few test runs around the airfield. He swept close to the onlookers below and laughed as he flew by. The others were not amused.

Once comfortable, he made the journey to the Kitab a couple of days later. He saw the various towns and weaved in and out of the dense bush along the river. Nobody saw him, however, due to the brilliant stealth technology. By nightfall, he saw the Port of Lub and flew through without detection. En route, he could see groups of people and homes dotted along the terrain. Lights twinkled in various areas. As he got closer, the region became more mountainous. He nearly hit a jutting rock but was able to clear it just in time. Fortunately, no one detected him along the way. The directions were perfect, like playing a video game in the arcade. He spotted the factory. He could see lights shining through the small windows. This was quite an imposing structure. Mahlpatrol were stationed on the perimeter. So far, no one saw him. As he entered, he detected the Transcript housed in a crate ready for sealing. He turned on the laser, which was the only piece of equipment detected by those below. He quickly stole the crate and flew back eastward. By now the Mahlpatrol had seen him and started firing, but they were too late. Once the unit was within the craft and the laser turned off, he was undetectable once again. Moch started to run out of gas not far from the factory. *Those stupid engineers*, he thought. They didn't calculate the amount of gas needed for the distance. He managed to land the plane and climbed out. The craft self-destructed quickly and silently. *Quite impressive*, he thought.

He retrieved the crate from the wreckage and took out the plastic case housing the Transcript, and then fled to the woods. The disintegration of the craft was swift and it continued to evade detection. He hid in the woods among the damp trees. The leaves were dangling lazily from the moisture. He felt cold from the previous night's rain. He cursed his predicament. Just then, he heard several patrols walking nearby. As he ran to escape them, he stumbled upon a small opening in the brush that led to a small pit hidden underground.

CHAPTER 3

The Retsel match was scheduled for the next day and preparations were running smoothly. Maklober was deep in paperwork when his supervisor, Lieutenant William F. Laerm ("Billy"), stormed in. "Goddamn it! That weasel Moch got out on a technicality."

"What?" screamed Maklober.

"You heard me, some group called the Directors got him out on a technicality. He's free to go."

"I don't believe it. After all these months of surveillance and finally capture, that's it, we just have to let him go?"

"Yeah!"

"That really sucks! Where is he now?"

"Who the hell knows? Probably out of the country by now."

"Is there any way to bring him back?"

"No," said Billy thoughtfully, calming down. "We just have to wait until he commits another crime. This time we'll have to make sure we cross every 't' and dot every 'i'."

"I thought we had on this case," said Maklober.

"So did I, but this group has some pretty sharp lawyers."

"So, what are you going to do?" asked Maklober.

"Don't worry about that, I'll get to the bottom of this. It's a frickin' embarrassment. Get back to work. We have other cases to solve."

Maklober thought about this for a while. He lit up a cigar, which he usually reserved for times of deep reflection. Moch eluded him this time, before Maklober could really learn about him. *What or who is this Moch?* he wondered. He wanted to ponder the details of the case further, but knew there was no time. Just as he was about to open up another case, he remembered that Moch was an unusually gifted pilot and could navigate anywhere, even the dreaded Kitab. He opened Moch's report and skimmed over some of the historical detail that elaborated on Moch's childhood. By the time he was a teenager he had grown to six feet and weighed about 160 pounds. He had rugged good looks, with a chiseled jaw and dimple in his chin. He had a V-shaped body to match. Maklober snorted. *Good looks and a criminal mind*, he thought.

Reading further, Maklober learned that Moch had trained in various martial arts and was a pilot. He later lived with the Security Council as a guest for a couple of years, training with the warriors. While there, he learned the ways of escaping detection. He eventually ascended to the level of master and was asked to join the security force.

Maklober paused and wondered what made Moch become a mercenary. Could there be a connection with the Retsel match? The various criminal organizations where Moch worked as a spy were detailed in the report. Maklober was happy that he was not the only one Moch left in the dust. Moch had been on the run from various branches of governments but always managed to escape into oblivion each time anyone got close to him.

"A man like that will never be out of work," Maklober reflected. "The skills he has are in demand by the underworld." The thought irritated Maklober.

He thumbed through the rest of Moch's file and found what he needed. He decided to pursue him there. He raced out of his office to tell Billy. When he approached, he saw that Billy was on the phone, involved in a rather heated discussion. At first, Maklober hesitated, but then he decided to go in. He sat down sheepishly and waited. He needed time to collect his thoughts.

Maklober and Billy had a special relationship dating back several years. As a child, Maklober always wanted to find out the truth about people. He was a natural detective. He remembered Billy showing him around the police station and the criminology lab and introducing him to the officers one summer when Maklober was still in high school. Maklober was so grateful that he vowed he would return one day as an officer. The detectives were amused and played along. Little did anyone know that Maklober would actually keep his word. Billy had taken him under his wing and nurtured him to his present position. Many of the detectives had since retired, shifted to part time work, or pursued academic pursuits teaching criminology at the college.

Maklober was finding it hard to wait. Billy finally hung up and slowly regained his composure.

"What is it, Maklober?" he asked.

Maklober thought for a minute, wishing secretly to find out about the cryptic telephone conversation, but knew better. Instead, he said rather cheerfully, "Boss, I have an idea. I want to take a few days of vacation after the Retsel match tomorrow."

"Why, for Christ's sake?"

"I have a hunch."

Billy stopped and looked at Maklober. "Well don't tell me. I don't want to know, right now anyway. Just stay out of trouble. Make sure everything is squared away at the match tomorrow before you leave," he said, seeming calmer. "Meanwhile, I'm going to find out just who the hell these Directors are and why they want to free someone like Moch in the first place."

"If we're going to bring down this group, we will definitely need Moch to testify," agreed Maklober.

He went home that night and packed his suitcase. He had read about the Kitab as a child but never visited. He didn't have occasion to go there, even as a detective, as their security force was very talented and handled their own problems. Furthermore, there was a mutual agreement not to inspect the defense arsenals and capabilities of each other's security forces.

***

Once the great hall was cleared following the Retsel match, Maklober went out and saw that things had calmed down a bit. He announced to the dispersing crowd that the paramedics were on their way and then lied by saying that the Retsel match would have to be replayed or postponed. That appeased everyone for the moment. He maintained communication, however, with his assistant via cell phone. Once satisfied that his crew was in charge, Maklober returned to his office but maintained constant communication. Chaych was taken to the hospital. Libertarian University officials demanded that, if possible, the match be completed at the hospital. The judges reluctantly agreed and took the Retsel board under cover to the hospital. Yarmin had already left before he could talk with her.

Maklober then went to the library after finishing up some paperwork at the office and prior to departing to review the literature on the Kitab. To date, the only information available was that provided by Lewy forty years ago. Maklober pored over the material diligently. Perhaps this doctor would be able to help him with the geographical perspectives.

Of special interest to Maklober was the description of the Port of Lub. This was their main port for transport of commodities within the region. There was no communication with the outside world except at the border between the Kitab and other half of the island. As a means of demarcation, the Kitabians constructed a stony arch that was anchored on each side of the river banks in the shape of a square with two horizontal posts aligned in parallel on top. One could fly through it at high speeds to avoid radar or course along the waterway on a motorized boat with low horsepower. This led to the main marketplace. Maklober thought that surely this would have been closed or else guarded very diligently. He thought about speaking with the author, Lewy, but quickly dismissed it as he felt that he would endanger him by making Lewy privy to his travel plans. Yarmin would also have to be kept in the dark on this one. To make sure, though, he called her and told her that he would be out of town for a few days on official police business. That night, he received a call from Yarmin on his landline but didn't pick up the phone. He didn't want to complicate matters further.

***

A few days after submitting the plans of his aircraft to the Directors and a day prior to the Retsel match, Lewy was sitting in his office reading the morning paper. The notorious criminal, Moch, had been liberated from prison without any reason. Lewy had never heard of this man and wondered why the newspaper would cover such a story. He read on with interest and learned that Moch had attempted to fly into the Kitab previously but was caught and placed in their custody. He somehow escaped using cyberspace technology that was foreign to the Kitab. The paper didn't go into any more detail on how he accomplished this feat. Lewy read about how detective Maklober of the Wellen police had caught him outside of the Kitab and was preparing to fill out the paperwork to allow prosecution to proceed. The Superiors wanted him tried and imprisoned. The particulars of Moch's release were not stated in the paper; just that he was let go on a technicality. Lewy wasn't satisfied with this explanation and called up a friend at the newspaper.

"What's the real story?" asked Lewy.

His friend was the co-investigator on the piece. "I can't say much, Lewy. I don't want panic to break out in Wellen. Suffice it to say the people are safe. Moch is notorious but to date hasn't harmed families. He is more interested in corporations."

"That's a relief, but I still want to know why he was released," said Lewy.

"Why are you so interested in this case?" asked the journalist. "This doesn't pertain to your work."

"I can't say. I just have a personal interest in this matter," said Lewy.

"Okay, but you will have to keep this under wraps or I'll be fired," said the journalist.

Lewy could hear the seriousness in his voice. "Agreed," said Lewy.

The friend continued, "Apparently, there is this group called the Directors who manipulated the system. They need Moch for some mission. I couldn't find out any more from my sources."

Lewy stood up, sweating nervously. He clenched the phone and said, "That's all I needed to know. I can take it from here."

His friend said, "If you know something, Lewy, please let me know."

By now, Lewy was growing impatient. He tried to remain calm. "It's just a hunch, but if it pans out, you won't need me to tell you. Your sources will find out way ahead of time," he said.

"You're worrying me, Lewy," his friend said.

"Trust me on this one," said Lewy.

"Okay, but be careful."

Lewy didn't want to place his friend's family in danger. He didn't trust the Directors and feared that they would harm his friend. Lewy now reasoned that the Directors sprung Moch from jail to fly the aircraft. The only logical place would be the Kitab, especially as Moch had knowledge of the terrain. But why?

CHAPTER 4

The morning after the Retsel match, Maklober awoke early and got ready. He had packed the night before and organized his business affairs. He ate a light breakfast while standing and glanced at the newspaper. He put down his piece of toast and grabbed a hold of the front page. In bold print, the headlines stated that Chaych in a stunning move won the match and Sci Tech University would close. Maklober read on. Chaych was undergoing further testing. Sci Tech was protesting the entire process but the judges' decision was final. He wondered why no one called him. He found his cell phone and learned that he inadvertently turned it off in the library. He turned it back on and saw that his assistant and Yarmin left voice messages about Chaych. Maklober was relieved to hear that his efforts weren't done in vain. After breakfast, he called for a cab to take him down to the river. The driver made light conversation, mostly about Chaych. Maklober played along and tried to remain inconspicuous. The driver had just moved to Wellen from Australia. He was studying biology at the university and drove a cab part-time for pocket money. They arrived at the dock in good time. Maklober wished him good luck and scrambled out of the car.

There was a flurry of activity. Tourists and dock workers were attempting to stay out of each other's way. He located the travel office, a small, nondescript space in a small building. There was a big sign hanging outside that simply read *Travel* in bright letters. This was on a busy corner of the dock. He made his way through the myriad of people and eventually entered through the small, narrow doorway. There were some people seated and others standing. The office was small with two desks. There were photographs on the walls of sights around the world. Brochures were lying haphazardly on a table and also hanging in a rack on the wall. It was a hot day and tempers were short. A fan was whirring away in one corner, which at least provided some comfort. One man was yelling at the workers about something. Maklober was preoccupied with his mission. He would have intervened if this escalated further, but fortunately they were able to resolve the issue amicably. He didn't want to blow his cover. He carried his badge in case. This time, however, he left his gun at home. The Kitab would imprison him if he was caught carrying a concealed weapon.

Maklober stood in the slow-moving line. After what seemed like eternity, he finally sat down at the next available desk. Amber, a bubbly redhead, greeted him cheerfully.

"What are you so happy about?" asked Maklober. "It's blistering hot outside and you've got a bunch of irate customers."

"One more day of this bullshit, then it's my turn for vacation," she said glibly.

"That sounds good; going anywhere exciting?"

"Not really, I just want to lie on a beach somewhere."

"I hear you."

She was quite attractive, thought Maklober. As he was on a mission, he quickly came back to reality.

"How can I help you?" she asked.

"I would like a ticket to Quine, please."

"You know, I've never been there," she said. "I've heard it's a quaint little town, though."

Despite the fan, sweat was forming on Maklober's forehead and his lower eyelids were starting to sag.

He perked up enough to say, "I haven't been there either. I'll let you know."

"I'd like that," she said. "Look me up after you return. Perhaps we could talk about it over dinner."

He received his ticket for the riverboat that normally takes tourists to the Kitab. He thanked her and quickly turned to leave before she got too personal.

"Have a nice trip," she said as he walked away.

"Thanks," he said.

Maklober was waiting in the departure lounge, hoping to stay anonymous, but unfortunately was seated next to a big, burly Wellenite.

After about five minutes, Maklober knew his whole life story. His name was Mark. He was in sales and was going to the Kitab on vacation. He was planning to meet his wife a day later as she had to work another day; last minute's notice. Maklober tried to keep the conversation light. Mark did not take the hint.

"So what's your name, my friend?" asked Mark.

Maklober said his name was Jack and that he worked as a clerk on the docks.

"I'm actually getting off at the next port, Lamin, which is on the way to Quine, to visit a sick relative," said Maklober.

"I'm sorry to hear that," said Mark.

"Thanks," said Maklober.

Luckily, Mark didn't inquire further. When they boarded the ship, Maklober tried to sit elsewhere, but the man found him and quickly sat in the adjoining seat. The rest of the journey was agonizing. Fortunately, their conversation did not attract others to join in. This is typically what happens in these situations. *Before you know it, everyone is involved like one big, happy family*, thought Maklober.

After a several hour ride, Maklober got off at Lamin. Mark was sad to see him go.

"It's too bad we can't meet up in the Kitab," said Mark.

"I don't think it will work out," said Maklober.

"Hey, how about we get together back in Wellen?" said Mark.

"I can't make any promises."

They exchanged phone numbers anyway. Maklober gave him a fake number—it was the number for the local psychiatric facility.

He immediately went to the dock and inquired into small motorboat rentals. Initially, he tried to play the dumb tourist, but saw that this wasn't getting him anywhere. He wanted to remain discreet as there were other customers in the store, but couldn't maintain his demeanor. Maklober lost his patience and demanded to speak with the owner.

"I am the owner," said the man across the counter. He was an older man, an ex-sailor built like a brick house with strong, muscular arms. He was wearing a short sleeve shirt rolled up to his shoulder. Maklober could make out a partially hidden tattoo of an anchor over his left deltoid. When he spoke, he squinted, furrowed his eyebrows, and pursed his lips. He held his arms out to the side as if steadying himself on a boat.

"Whaddya really want?" the owner barked.

There were other customers in the store, so Maklober requested more privacy. They went into his office; a small space with a steel desk and a chair. There were pictures of sailboats hanging unevenly on the walls.

"Okay," said the owner with a gravelly voice, "I'm busy. What is it?"

Maklober flashed his badge and said, "I'm in Lamin on official police business from Wellen and am in pursuit of a notorious criminal."

The sailor squinted at the badge and said, "Who? And where is he?"

"I can't tell you the details, but I think he is either here in Lamin or on his way to the Kitab," said Maklober.

"I can't rent you a boat to go the Kitab," he said, shaking his head. "They will have my head."

"Don't worry," said Maklober. "I only plan to use the boat to get to the Port of Lub."

"Where?" asked the sailor.

"This is the entry point to the Kitab."

"I've never heard of it."

"Only a few people outside of the Kitab know of it," said Maklober.

"Been a sailor all my life and never came across it; don't believe it."

"If I were you," said Maklober, "I would forget about it for it will only land you in trouble."

"I'll think about it," said the sailor.

"Back to the matter at hand," said Maklober. "I'll leave the boat at the entryway, hidden from sight, and enter on foot. Don't worry, if there is any damage, I'll pay for it."

"You betta believe it, mister. Just in case, I'll need collateral," said the sailor.

"Here's my badge. It would only get me into trouble anyway. I'll pick it up on the way back," said Maklober.

"Okay, whaddya need?" asked the sailor.

"A small boat with low horsepower; the journey is about twenty miles."

"That will take a couple of days at best," said the sailor.

"I know, but I don't want to attract any attention," said Maklober. "I need to be as quiet as possible and blend in with the local environment."

"In that case, you'll need a couple of tanks of gas."

"Bill it to the Wellen Police Department, attention Captain Laerm."

With that, they got the boat ready for sail. The sailor showed Maklober how to operate the craft. Maklober loaded the boat with basic survival supplies in the event he was captured. He did not want any high-tech gadgets or weapons. In fact, he turned off his cell phone but kept it in case of an emergency. He was simply going on a camping expedition. The sailor told him prior to loading up the boat to go to a camping store across the street to pick up a tent and other supplies. It was early afternoon. There was a small breeze, which helped to mitigate the blistering heat. Once Maklober felt comfortable with the controls, he thanked the man and set sail. He waited for the tourist ship to leave first, then embarked on the twenty-mile journey to the Port of Lub, coursing along the smaller waterways. Unfortunately, he could not ask anyone whether the port still existed, as this would betray his mission. There were no charted maps for guidance. He only knew the general direction and relied heavily on his compass. Along the way, the river was quiet. Most of the banks were covered in deep foliage. From time to time, he could see farmers in the distant fields. No one detected him and probably would not care even if they did. He wore simple clothes and a straw hat. The water was calm, with occasional perturbations. The weather was cooperating. The animal life was small and nonthreatening. He brought some army rations with him and set up camp halfway. He slept in the brush and lit a small fire for warmth. Sleep came quickly but he was restless.

It was nightfall the next day when he arrived within radar distance at the Port of Lub. He stopped the motor and paddled over to the shore. He wasn't sure if anyone saw or heard him. He waited for about half an hour, then got out and surveyed the land around him. He hid the boat in the bushes and thought about his next move. He observed the pattern of river traffic and watched for patrol activity into the next day and night. He continued to eat army rations and local fruit. Water was plentiful as the natural streams were untouched and pristine. He set up camp and slept till the next morning, when he was awakened by the sound of a helicopter far in the distance. He could make out the Kitab's insignia; two interlocking gray pentagons slightly skewed on a white background. He wondered if they had spotted him. After awhile, the helicopter flew away; Maklober figured it was probably just a routine patrol flight. There was no river traffic or ground activity. During the day, he took cover along the shoreline, paddling short distances and then stopping to avoid detection. He could see the Kitabian mountain range looming in the distance from the brush below. That night, he decided to paddle closer to the port. As he arrived, he heard a lot of activity and saw several boats and lights. Mahlpatrol were stationed throughout. The difference in security between Wellen and the Kitab was palpable. He was quite impressed with the organization of the security teams. They were perfectly positioned to look inconspicuous but at the same time everyone knew of their presence.

There seemed to be a huge shipment arriving. As he got closer, he saw the Port of Lub in the distance, just as described by Lewy. He carefully rowed through. *So far, so good*, he thought. He could make out a small landing on the shore. He climbed out of the boat and made a small splash. Fortunately, no one heard him. He waited a few minutes, in case, then hid the boat in the woods on shore. Once secured, he crept along the shoreline, encountering small animals. They were a nuisance as they darted around him. Once he cleared the brush, he found stable footing on the dry dock. He could see the wear and tear on the concrete landing from centuries of water erosion and neglect. In the water, there were waste products probably washed ashore from the port. Tires and rotting wood cluttered the small beach. This then led to the main dock, which was more stable in appearance. The pavement looked relatively new. Maklober suddenly realized that he would be spotted in his clothes. The workers and townspeople wore uniforms. He would be out of place even as a tourist.

Once on the dock he spotted a laundry truck, and he carefully peeked into the cab and saw that no one was in the front seat. Maklober made his way to the rear doors and looked through a small opening in the slightly ajar door. He saw large bags tied with rope. He quickly opened the door and grabbed a bag, adeptly untied the rope, and saw dirty uniforms. He hastily grabbed one and ran out, forgetting to tie the bag. He then ran to a dark corner by one of the warehouses and donned the pale yellow outfit with the Kitab insignia embroidered over the left breast, and slowly walked into the marketplace. Out of the corner of his eye he saw the driver of the laundry truck return, throw his load in the back, close the door, and drive off. Maklober was lucky this time. He tried to blend in as much as possible, but he was lost, with no maps or directions.

Maklober saw the workers loading and unloading huge crates off the barges along the dock. At equidistant points corresponding to each warehouse entrance, there was a waste receptacle. One was filled to the brim with newspapers read during the day then discarded. He took one out and intently stared at the print. One story in particular caught his eye. The headlines stated that an intruder was spotted in the northern corner of the Kitab. He had apparently stolen software needed for the Superiors to run the government. The economy came to a standstill. The intruder was somehow able to elude the detection of the Mahlpatrol. Maklober snorted. It had to be Moch. Maklober looked around with his trained policeman's eye and saw several groups of security guards in the distance, stationed at various points along the dock. He knew he would have to be very careful. The papers didn't go into much detail. Maklober reasoned this was for security reasons. No one was permitted to leave their villages unless for work.

While he was walking and reading the article, he ran into a worker who was dressed in a similar uniform. *He looked harmless enough,* thought Maklober. He knew that the Kitabians were tight-lipped and would not pry into another's business. Maklober was only interested in Moch at this point. Luckily, the Kitabian accent was similar to Wellen, except in the small villages where subtle nuances could be detected. That simple fact alone could betray you. Maklober tried to speak as succinctly as possible to keep his accent neutral.

"What's your take on this intruder?" asked Maklober.

"I don't actually know, but from what I hear, this man flew into the Kitab in a vehicle that was stealth-like and is in hiding for now," said the worker nervously as he glanced right and left, looking for any guards.

"That's what I heard too," said Maklober, adding, "It's time to get back to work."

Before the worker had a chance to become too friendly, Maklober raced off. He did not know where to search, but knew that he had to catch a ride on one of the ships headed to the northern part of the Kitab. He read the schedule of departures and saw that one of the ships was leaving in the next hour. He quickly spotted the ship and ran under cover to try to stow away. He saw a gathering of workers and followed them into the cargo hold. He found a small hiding area. He knew this would only be temporary. There was another team of workers who would sail with the ship. Unfortunately, he could see that they wore a different uniform; gray with black buttons and a pocket over the left breast. The Kitabian insignia was sewn just above the pocket in white letters. He was running out of time and needed to find a new uniform, but didn't want to draw attention to himself. He saw two ramps on the ship, once for exiting and the other for entering. He went over to the exiting side and observed the process. The workers who had returned from their journey walked to the warehouse by the ship and went in. Maklober followed them and hid by the side of the building under a small window. He then stood on his tiptoes and peeked inside. He saw a row of lockers. The workers threw their uniforms in a bin and changed into a similar uniform that Maklober was wearing. Once they cleared out, Maklober went in and stole one of the uniforms. Fortunately, there were no names, just the insignia above the breast pocket. He then snuck his way out made his way up to the passenger hold and joined the ranks leading up the entrance ramp.

CHAPTER 5

As Lewy had no family and did not fear for his life, he decided to visit the Kitab after so many years to help to capture Moch. He had no other commitments. He was about six feet tall and quite fit. He had a full head of graying hair and a small goatee. His skin betrayed his age from the late nights working on autopsies,

As an outlet, he engaged in training sessions weekly with a local master and then went to the Security Council's base every summer to enroll in their two-week course. All he knew was that he wanted to stop the Directors and clear his name. Surely, news would eventually get out that he was the one who designed the aircraft.

He told his institution that he had to take off a few days to pursue independent study. The center was used to this from Lewy as he would from time to time spring these spontaneous breaks.

Anyway, the lab was running smoothly. His assistants were on autopilot for now. Lewy did not relate his intentions to the local police force. Instead, he called a friend in the diplomatic corps that was attached to the Kitab.

***

Ambassador Joseph Barnes went through the ranks of the consulate general's office, first as an assistant traveling to various parts of the world for four-year stints. Later, he rose to the rank of consulate general, and then ambassador. When his cousin died mysteriously at the age of sixty, his remains were taken to Lewy's lab for study. The family was extremely dismayed over his death and wanted to discover the etiology as soon as possible. They called Joseph, who personally spoke with Lewy and requested that he perform the autopsy. Joseph was impressed with his demeanor and proficiency.

At the postmortem examination, they stood hunched over the brain of Joseph's cousin. At gross inspection, there was only slight atrophy, but there was a curious spongy texture to the brain. When Joseph asked Lewy what he thought, Lewy said, "I suspect that this represents prion disease."

"In English, please."

"This looks like mad cow disease."

"What? But how is that possible?"

"Sometimes mutations can occur and lead to this form of degeneration in the brain. I'll call you tomorrow once the sections are ready."

Joseph arrived at ten o'clock the next morning after a long night with the family. The fatigue and worry were visible on his face. Lewy reviewed the slides with Joseph on the multi-headed teaching microscope; the slides confirmed his diagnosis.

Joseph was appreciative and told him to call him if he ever needed a favor along diplomatic lines. It was now that time.

***

Maklober escaped detection and safely stowed aboard the large ship headed for the northern part of the Kitab. For warmth, he huddled around the massive chimney on the ship's upper deck. The cargo levels were unsafe given the level of security. They were also cold. He hid among the workers who had also found their way to this spot on the deck for warmth. The ship was primarily intended for cargo. The workers were shuttled back and forth along the upper deck, as there was no passenger space. Papers were typically not needed. The Mahlpatrol felt that these workers weren't educated or brave enough to cause any harm or breach in security. This was fortunate for Maklober, as he was surprised that no one came around to check for passes. The uniform sufficed. He remained to himself so as to not attract attention. Once he settled down, he realized that he hadn't eaten anything since entering the Port of Lub. Luckily, he had one last bar of army rations. He slowly removed it from his pocket.

"Hey, what have you got there?" asked one of the workers.

"This?" said Maklober. "Nothing, just a piece of candy."

"How about sharing with the rest of us?" said the worker. He was a burly, unshaven man who stunk like the sea. He was missing his two front teeth and spoke with a gravelly voice.

Before this got out of hand, Maklober whispered to him.

"If you want some, come this way. I don't want the others to know; more for us, if you know what I mean."

The worker understood. They went to the side of the ship. Maklober was concerned that this worker would blow his cover by drawing too much attention to him. Furthermore, the rations were from Lamin.

"Okay, give me a piece already," said the worker.

"Just a minute," said Maklober.

The worker was getting impatient and was about to lunge for the rations. At that moment, Maklober darted around to the back of the worker, grabbed him in a wrestling hold, and crushed his trachea in the process. The man gave out a brief gasp and then went limp. Maklober then draped him over the wall and slid him down the side. He landed in the water with a small splash. The sound was muffled by the wake of the boat and the churning of the propellers below. Maklober massaged his shoulder, an old wrestling injury. The worker had grabbed hold of this shoulder while Maklober was lifting him over the wall. Maklober stayed by the side of the ship for awhile. There were faint murmurs, but otherwise, no cause for alarm. Once he thought the coast was clear, he returned to his spot by the chimney, but first finished the rations.

The rest of the overnight journey was uneventful. He was even able to catch a few hours of sleep. He was awakened by shouts from the workers. They were close to shore and preparations were underway to start unloading the cargo. Upon arrival it was dawn, but still dark enough to escape. The landscape was mountainous and the vegetation scarce. The dock was quite large and formidable. He made his way to one of the exit points and took cover. Once the workers started to disembark, he joined the ranks. They were to assemble at the dock and await further instructions. It was at this point that Maklober slipped away and took cover in one of the warehouses. There wasn't much activity. There were several thousand pallets of boxes that he reasoned were stored for eventual transport. He suddenly realized how hungry he had become. Quietly, he opened up one of the boxes but found that they were pieces of machinery. He then hid for awhile and when he could, he slithered around the pallets and saw a grouping of boxes labeled "perishable." He found some nutritional supplements in one of the boxes intended for the workers. He quickly and quietly closed the box and tucked it away among the myriad of supplies. The few rations he took wouldn't be missed. Throughout the day, he stayed undercover and risked opening the package of rations when he saw that no one was around.

He waited till nightfall then found where the workers were housed. He slept under their cover and followed them the next day to the factory. Upon entering, there was quite a buzz in the air about someone stealing the Transcript. Security was tightened and all were searched. Maklober snuck away in time and hid in another warehouse.

***

The Mahlpatrol had swooped down on the entire Kitab in a force that no one had ever seen before. The hunt was on for Moch.

Maklober knew that he couldn't stay in the warehouse for long before getting caught. There was a door at the rear of the warehouse. He ran out cautiously and headed for the woods that led away from the river. He could hear the Mahlpatrol and cries from the workers behind him. He darted through the dense underbrush, trying to find solid footing. He could hear the snapping of twigs and tree branches, which had formed a carpet underneath him. He followed the makeshift path through the trees, trying to avoid ground cover and small animals at the same time. He had come across a rock formation rising above the terrain. In the clearing, he saw a small furry animal enter a small opening between the rocks and then curiously disappear. He followed him in and saw that the opening led to a cave. He slowly entered and saw barely legible drawings on the stone walls. There were areas of water trickling down the sides, making the ground cold and moist. There was a stale odor. The small animal had scurried back outside in fear. To Maklober's amazement, he saw Moch huddled up in the darkness holding on to a small plastic case.

CHAPTER 6

Moch whispered in bewildered excitement, "What the hell are you doing here, Maklober?"

Maklober was taken aback by the shock of seeing Moch. Once he came to his senses, he said, "Actually, trying to find you. I had a feeling you would end up back here on some hare-brained mission. Before I haul your ass back into custody, I just want to know, who is it for this time?" asked Maklober.

Moch shifted position. He was growing uncomfortable. "Not so fast, cowboy. We're in the Kitab now. You have no jurisdiction here," he said. Maklober pondered his options, and before he could speak, Moch said, "You'll never guess."

"You're right, I have no idea," said Maklober. He relaxed somewhat, knowing that they weren't going anywhere for the moment; at least not without a plan.

"The Directors," said Moch.

"Who?" asked Maklober.

"You mean, you never heard of them?"

"No, who are they?" Maklober was intently listening by now. He had been a policeman for years and silently scolded himself for never hearing of this group.

"They are this super-conservative group of alumni from Sci Tech University who by all means does not want Libertarian University to prevail."

"How?"

"They have this vague hope that by stealing this software program they can somehow take over control of the Kitab and then leverage their position to reopen Sci Tech."

"Brilliant!" said Maklober. "So simple in form."

"What are you talking about?" asked Moch.

Maklober didn't say anything. He was reveling in his discovery.

"Twisted, ain't it?" said Moch.

"You are simply a pawn to carry out this service," said Maklober. "Do you really think they will keep you on board if they succeed? You are dispensable, my friend!"

"Won't the Security Council or Australia step in?" asked Moch.

"I doubt it," said Maklober. "They usually don't interfere with individual governments. As long as global security isn't breached, they will likely just simply observe. Australia won't care either."

"What are you going to do now, Maklober, parade me out there in front of the entire Kitab and Mahlpatrol? If we get caught, we're both dead. The Mahlpatrol has no mercy," said Moch as he shifted position on the hard ground, growing tired of the dialogue.

Maklober shrugged. "I'll take my chances. Once I turn you into the Mahlpatrol and return the Transcript, I can then work along diplomatic lines to take you back into Wellen's custody.

"Easier said than done," said Moch.

As Maklober was leaning up against the wall, Moch lay down the Transcript on the cold ground and suddenly sprang up and delivered a quick kick to Maklober's left knee. He went down swiftly, holding his knee in agony. "You ain't going to catch me, Maklober. Mark my words," said Moch as he picked up the case housing the Transcript and fled the cave.

Maklober yelled out with a creaky voice from the pain, "You're mine, Moch. I'll get you the next time." He could hear Moch laughing in the distance then everything went silent.

***

Moch ran through the woods along a similar path that Maklober took, taking care to avoid animals and trying not to draw too much attention by cracking the carpet of twigs and branches underneath. At times he encountered small patrols of security. On one occasion, he had to restrain a single patrolman. He subdued him but decided to spare his life. He covered him by the brush and continued onward. He finally saw the ship. Security was all over the dock.

***

When Maklober was awakened an hour later by some small animal, he realized Moch had gone. He was upset that Moch got the better of him. *That moron,* thought Maklober. He smiled to himself as he suspected that alone, Moch would surely be caught. The Mahlpatrol would catch him and then good luck. He now had to think of getting back without risking capture and ending up in jail for trespassing. He tried to get up but suddenly felt a bolt of pain over his knee where Moch had kicked him. He sat back down in agony, cursing Moch. After massaging his swollen knee, he got up and hobbled outside. After a few minutes of walking, the pain started to subside. He had a large bruise but could move his knee. He slowly made his way through the woods back to the river.

CHAPTER 7

"Joseph, this is Lewy."

Joseph's face lit up and said, "Well hello, Doc. It's been a long time. How can I help you?"

Lewy was relieved that Joseph remembered him. After the usual pleasantries, Lewy lowered his voice, relaxed his face, and said in a serious tone, "Listen, Joseph, I want to go the Kitab to warn the Mahlpatrol of a certain criminal."

Joseph said rather calmly, "I'm well ahead of you on this one."

Lewy paused a moment on the other end of the phone in bewilderment. "You mean you already know?"

"Yeah, the scuttlebutt is that an intruder flew in to the northern factory, the Tangle, and stole software required to run their government. They call it the Transcript."

"What!" cried out Lewy.

"Yeah, he flew in undetected and stole this software program using a laser."

"Joseph, I have to confess something. I was forced to design this craft for a group known as the Directors. As it turns out, this group consists of leaders in our own society that has now turned completely self-serving. They were to fly this craft into the Kitab, but I had no idea it was to steal something so important."

"Doc, you should have told me sooner. I could have alerted the authorities."

"I had no choice. They threatened to harm my staff's families. Can you help me?"

"Okay, you sit tight, Doc. A limousine will be there shortly to pick you up."

Lewy joined Joseph at the heliport. They flew to the Kitab. En route, no one spoke. Upon arrival, they were met by Captain Krom, members of the Mahlpatrol, and agents of the Superiors. Everything was explained. Lewy recognized some of the older members of the Mahlpatrol from his student days.

Captain B. L. Krom was a new recruit when Lewy first met him forty years ago. Lewy was impressed with his fortitude and wisdom at such a young age. Captain Krom had showed Lewy around the quarters at that time and explained their operation as much as was permissible. Lewy himself joined in one of their training exercises. *Quite rigorous,* he thought. Lewy knew hand-to-hand combat, as he was a student of various forms of martial arts since childhood. He had not known that each member of the Mahlpatrol was expert in the art as well. He definitely met his match that day. Krom eventually ascended to the rank of captain and became quite a hero.

"Lewy, are you involved with this?" asked Krom suddenly.

"Tragically, yes, I'm afraid."

They all drove to one of many small airports that dotted the Kitab and flew north in a small aircraft to the factory. Upon landing, they met with the Superiors and explained the whole story once again. They were, needless to say, quite outraged.

"In which direction did the pilot fly?" asked Lewy.

"Southeast. We tracked him for about a mile and then lost him."

"I have an idea," said Lewy. "Let's take the trail along the river as we may assume he landed."

"How can you make that assumption?" asked Krom.

"In designing the aircraft, we had to estimate the distance in order to calculate the size of the fuel tank. As I figured this project was for illegal means, I wanted to make sure that the perpetrators would get caught without their suspecting us of foul play."

"Strong work," said Joseph. The men waited for Krom's reaction.

"Okay, all available men with the Doc," said Krom.

They ran along the banks of the river trying to locate Moch. Lewy recalled some of the terrain from his exploration of the Kitab as a young student. Everything remained the same. The Kitab hadn't changed. One of the men heard sounds in the distance. They came across the patrolman that Moch had subdued.

"He's still alive," said Lewy, quickly checking his vital signs.

He was swiftly taken to the local hospital, but he wasn't able to offer much information as he was taken by surprise. Further on, some members of the Mahlpatrol were rejoicing that they stumbled upon a lead. When Lewy and others arrived, they learned that there was a small makeshift camp in a cave between the rock formations.

"How did you find this place so quickly?" asked Lewy.

Krom said that the Mahlpatrol had designed small computerized animals a few years ago to patrol the outlying areas. "This cave is in one of the charted zones," he said.

"Was there anyone in the cave at the time?" asked Lewy.

"Yes, but the scout couldn't get a clear picture with its built-in camera," said Krom.

"Any sounds?"

"It sounded like a man in pain, but he left quickly and the scout couldn't keep up," said Krom.

"That's helpful at least. This was probably Moch, and he's hurt," said Lewy.

"Let's go," said Krom. The Mahlpatrol went to search the ships.

"I'd like to go too. I feel responsible," pleaded Lewy as he sheepishly looked at Krom and Joseph.

"You look healthy, but are you in shape for something like this?" said Joseph.

"Yeah, I've actually remained quite active physically, especially in the art of combat."

They decided that Lewy would team up with Ambassador Joseph Barnes and the Mahlpatrol to pursue Moch. Lewy knew this would be no small feat, but he needed to get close to the ships, and the Mahlpatrol offered him cover. He carefully thought out his options. He did not want to involve Joseph in his plans as he intended to pursue Moch independently. He thought the ambassador would only slow him down. He was a diplomat, not a warrior.

***

Moch managed to sneak aboard the ship the next night. The entrance ramp was heavily guarded. He waited for the right opportunity and found it when two workers got into a fight. Others called over the guards and Moch ran over to the unguarded ramp as fast as he could. He tucked the Transcript under his clothes. Lewy and Joseph had an

38

easier time and boarded the ship along with the security guards. The Superiors were still on the lookout for Moch and suspected that he escaped on one of the ships. They waited at the Port of Lub but did not see him.

***

Maklober recalled reading in Lewy's notes that there were two separate waterways in the Kitab. The most common was the one that tourists and guests of the government took. The other was less known and only then to the local inhabitants as the Sapere River. This was a massive river with wide banks and slow-flowing water. It coursed to the Port of Lub, though at one point tapered down and trickled to a land mass. The river resumed, but only after undergoing an arduous journey over the marshland. At the entry point of the river there was less regulation.

Maklober had managed to sneak aboard the same ship as Moch but could not take action for fear of getting caught. Maklober was bursting with anger. He wanted to catch Moch himself and take credit for turning him in rather than blowing the whistle. His ego was bruised. Once on board, he saw Moch in the shadows and was about to take the opportunity to catch him. At that moment, however, someone came into the cargo hold where he was hiding and Moch slipped out, giving a quick wave to Maklober.

At the next port, the city of Sylmon, he disembarked. He assumed that Moch would also take the less-traveled route, as he too knew the geography of the Kitab. Just as Maklober was following Moch's trail, a group of Mahlpatrol crossed his path. *Shit*, he thought. *I have to take cover now.* He hid in a busy warehouse at the dock and waited till evening. He hadn't seen Moch the entire day. If he were caught, he surely would have heard a huge outcry. As none came, he assumed that he escaped once again. *By now*, he thought, *Moch must be well on his way along the Sapere River.*

***

Moch arrived at the dock, out of breath. He was panting, trying to figure out how to get aboard the boat without drawing attention to himself. He hid alongside a container that had just been offloaded from one of the boats. Guards were posted everywhere and the streets were deserted. As he ran, he heard announcements over a public address system telling the townspeople to stay indoors. He saw a lone guard—with muscles protruding under his uniform as he carried his rifle—making his way toward the container.

The guard's expression was blank as he circled around the container. As the guard came closer, Moch turned around and approached him from behind. Swiftly and with the agility of a ninja, he grabbed him by the throat and crushed his trachea. The guard fell like a limp doll. His rifle landed softly on the ground. Moch left him by the side of the container. The container was right at the river's edge, so he guessed he could swim to the now departing boat. The other guards were making rounds elsewhere. When he saw his chance, he slipped into the water and swam as fast as he could to the side of the boat. He stayed clear of the propellers underneath. He spotted a ladder on the side facing away from the dock and climbed up the rungs, struggling with each movement from the fatigue in his calves. Once he reached the top, he draped himself across the rail and snuck his way down below. He saw a guard just as he was about to round a corner and ducked into a room filled with boxes. He took off his outer clothes to let them dry and hid behind the boxes. He felt safe for the moment. The Transcript was still intact. The plastic covering was waterproof.

***

At night, Maklober snaked his way to the Sapere. There was a small rowboat tied up near the river. It looked rather worn and loosely anchored to shore. There were no supplies or markers of identification. *This won't be missed*, he thought, and sailed downstream. There were no maps for guidance. Small white fish darted around the reddish rocks in the clear water. The banks of the river had dense underbrush, but from time to time he would pass by small villages. Each one appeared similar, at least from the river. Small boats were anchored to small piers that jutted out from the dense woods. These small villages seemed to be residential communities, as there was no substantial activity or commercial vehicles. Throughout the woods there were small recreational areas, though for now all was quiet. The Kitab imposed a curfew for everyone after dinner for fear of attacks in the woods. He did not know the nature of the attacks or the persons responsible. He dared to stop at one of the small docks along the river to relieve himself. As he got out, he noticed a rather eerie silence. There was nothing stirring. The trees were still with their leaves dangling wistfully. The evening sun filtered through openings in the woods, casting shadows on the water. The recreational areas were furnished only with a picnic table and a barbecue grill. He found a weathered and barely legible flyer lying on the ground. It said, "Beware of the Ti ..." He could not make out the rest. *Strange*, he thought. It sounded like an animal or thing was frightening the people. He did his duty and promptly got back into the boat. He kept the flyer and decided to inquire about it at the next opportunity. He slowly rowed downstream, keeping close to shore.

He came across the large city of Massa, where there was quite a great deal of activity. Workers were loading transport vehicles with supplies, destined for different parts of the Kitab. He got out of the boat and hid it in the underbrush. After scanning the area for about an hour, he cautiously walked to the city. As he arrived, he noted that all the homes were the same size and shape, in varying shades of gray. The color was a remarkable and indescribable hue and sheen. The inhabitants were also fairly uniform, like clones. He recalled Lewy's observations that the cities resembled the gray cells and white matter of the brain. The roads were primitive, with dogs and cats roaming freely in and out of the lush vegetation. This part of the Kitab was in many ways similar and also different from the rest. This linked the interior of the Kitab to the major waterways, including the final link back to the Port of Lub. As it was dark, he searched for a place to sleep.

***

Lewy and Joseph embarked on their journey back to the Port of Lub. They took the next daily ship reserved for guests and tourists. Joseph had stayed on board during the ship's scheduled stop. As they were getting underway, he went to Lewy's cabin to talk about their plans. To his surprise and anguish, Lewy wasn't there. He had disembarked at the Port of Lub alone. The Mahlpatrol learned that Lewy was not on board and mounted a search. They were quite disappointed in Joseph. He tried his best to keep diplomatic lines open but at this point was asked to leave. The Mahlpatrol had their work cut out for them.

***

At the City of Sylmon, where Moch and Maklober had initially disembarked, Lewy managed to sneak away and ran through the warehouse district. He would have to find his way to Massa. Lewy took cover in an abandoned building to plot out his next move. He roughly knew this part of the Kitab from his studies. He intended to help track down Moch to clear his own name. His memory of the Kitab's geography was somewhat sketchy at this point. He did not recall exactly how to reach the Sapere River. He attempted to blend in as much as possible—he was still wearing his clothes from Wellen. In observing the locals, he saw that they wore pale yellow uniforms with the Kitabian insignia embroidered on the breast pocket. He searched for a uniform but had no success. He waited undercover and ultimately saw a group of people walking toward another building. After about five minutes, they came back out with nicely starched uniforms. After they left, he darted over to the building and peered through a ground level window. There was a bin of soiled clothing. He had to find a way to get in and out without notice. He went back to his hiding place and waited. The same worker, who Lewy had seen earlier through the window, now appeared in the doorway and then walked to another building. His chance had come. Lewy raced back and first looked through the window. Once the coast was clear, he ran inside and stole a uniform. He dried the sweat on his forehead and returned to his hiding place. After changing into the uniform, he stashed his clothes behind a pallet of boxes. Once properly attired, he felt more confident, but Lewy still walked through the quiet streets as rapidly as possible. Fortunately, it was near nightfall and most of the inhabitants had retired to their homes. He ducked into a small store and asked for directions, discreetly. He was also aware of the nuances in accents and tried to imitate the locals. He spoke sparingly and tried to get as much information as possible. The owner of the store looked at him suspiciously, but figured he was one of those dirty sailors. He told Lewy to take the hourly bus that took workers to the docks. He thanked the man and swiftly made his way. He was cautious and remained suspicious that the man would alert the authorities. To ensure his safety, he hid behind the store for about an hour. As he saw no security patrols, he walked to the bus stop. He thought that by now the police would have surrounded the area. There were other workers huddled together at the stop. He walked up slowly and quietly to avoid attracting attention to himself. The bus arrived. They all marched in like sardines in a can. Once at the port, Lewy camped down in a warehouse and drifted off to sleep, thinking about his next move.

***

Maklober had walked quite a long way and was growing tired. He rested by the roadside near a tall tree. He could see a large town in the distance. Trucks were passing by him on a regular basis. He stayed a little longer and then walked inside the tree line alongside the road. As he approached, he saw a sign that read "Welcome to the Thalamian Villages." He recalled from his readings that this was a massive land mass that consisted of several towns, each contributing in their own way to not only survival of their own village but also to the entire Kitab. The villages were separated by a rail system known as the Grenzen Line. It was heavily used by the locals because of its ease, speed, and convenience. Lewy went to say in his chronicles that there were two sets of tracks going east-west, cutting a straight line through the villages. The locomotive was still powered by coal. There were six cars, one for the Mahlpatrol, three for passengers, and two for cargo and freight. The seats were rather uncomfortable, but most passengers only rode short distances. The majority stood, with quick exchanges at the various stops. There was a primitive and narrow service road that ran parallel to the train tracks. Only in unusual circumstances would one travel by car.

Maklober found a small clearing at the entry to the road and took cover. He caught a few hours of sleep in the brush. By morning, he was massaging his shoulder, an old wrestling injury. He looked around, and once secure that all was safe, made his way to the Grenzen Line. Just as he was about to leave, he felt a hand restraining his arm. He was about to fight back, but was quickly subdued. He started to yell out but he felt a hand coming over his mouth and someone whisper in his ear to shut up. Maklober tried to spin around but the man had a hold on his weak shoulder. His knee was also hurting him from the long walk. After a few seconds, the man said, "I'm going to let go, but please be quiet." Maklober was in agony by now and slowly turned around. His face was contorted in pain. As he relaxed, he looked at his captor more clearly and gathered his thoughts.

CHAPTER 8

"Who are you?" he said.

Lewy whispered, "I'm Dr. L. W. Gehirn, perhaps you've heard of me?"

"Are you the one who wrote about the Kitab forty years ago?"

"Yes, indeed."

"Well, how and why did you get here?" said Maklober.

"It's a long story and for now time is of the essence. I need your help and you need mine."

"No one knows I'm here, but does anyone know about you?"

Lewy replied, "Yeah, I originally came with the ambassador, but I managed to escape in the hopes of clearing my name. I want to catch Moch, for it was I who designed the aircraft."

"What?" said Maklober to restrain himself. "We'll both be captured for sure. The Mahlpatrol will be on the lookout for you and Moch, and I'll be caught in the process."

"Maklober, you need my help to navigate around these parts. Fortunately, no one knows you're here or what you look like. I have a friend, Papez, who lives in the first village to the south. He will help us."

"How can you be so sure?" asked Maklober.

"Once, long ago, I met him when he was a journalism student. I gave him information about our society and academic world. He was grateful and pledged to help me whenever I needed."

"That was forty years ago, though. How do you know he is still here?"

"Oh, I received a letter from him about two years ago. He no longer practices journalism. He is retired and lives in a forest outside the village as a recluse. No one bothers him now. I have an idea where he lives, but we'll have to be careful."

"Okay, Dr. Gehirn, we have to hurry, it's fast approaching daylight."

"Maklober, please call me Lewy, everyone does."

"Okay."

Before boarding the train, they waited and observed the activity. Some of the men were carrying lunch pails. They had dark circles under their eyes and unshaven faces. "It looks like they've come off a shift," said Lewy. "We'll be fine. We're already wearing uniforms. It looks like you haven't shaved in days anyway, Maklober," said Lewy.

"Thanks," said Maklober. They walked over to the train and boarded. They sat down and remained quiet. Fortunately no one took notice as this was a regular workday and everyone was scurrying along. When they reached the first station, there were Mahlpatrol guards all over the place.

"What now, Lewy?"

"Leave it up to me. We must disembark with the others and behave as they do. This is our only chance."

They walked confidently into the marketplace. After studying the various transportation options, they took a local bus to the countryside. The landscape was rather simple and uniform. Everyone had neat houses and manicured lawns. Once they reached the countryside, they were let off the bus, as this was the last stop. They then hiked about a mile along a gravel path in a vast forest until they reached a little dwelling. No one traveled the path with them. They could hear small animal sounds and birds rustling through the leaves. At the small house, there was smoke coming from the chimney.

"The serenity gives me the creeps," said Maklober softly.

"Papez must be home, but let's wait a few hours to make sure the coast is clear," said Lewy in a whisper. "I just want to make sure that no patrols come by. I don't want to endanger Papez."

While they were waiting, Maklober spoke with Lewy about his work and observations of the Kitab as a student. Their conversation was interrupted by the sound of a motor. They hid under some bushes and remained vigilant. They dared not speak. They saw a jeep with two guards carrying rifles. As the path ended at Papez's house, the guards stopped and waited for a few minutes, then turned around and drove back. After awhile, they could no longer hear the motor.

"That was close," said Maklober.

"I bet this is a regular occurrence," said Lewy.

"It was a good idea to wait out here. This way, we could see the timings of these patrols," said Maklober. As the day wore on, two more patrols came by, looked cursorily while sitting in the jeep, then turning around and returning the way they came.

"So far," Maklober whispered, "they haven't gotten out of their cars."

"That's fortunate for us, but we still have to be on the look out. We'll ask Papez later what typically happens with the patrols at night," said Lewy. The two men waited in the bush until early afternoon. They were growing hungry, but they held their ground.

"So what's the deal with Papez?" asked Maklober.

Lewy looked up to the clear blue sky and thought before he spoke. He then began to speak in a low voice. "About forty years ago, he reported rather liberally about the organization of the Kitab and was subsequently imprisoned. Due to good behavior, he was paroled with the one condition that he stop writing, and he was ordered to stay in the forest as a recluse. He was given a small pension and house. The Kitab censored his letters. He had no telephone or access to a computer. He only had a radio to connect with the outside world. Newspapers only consisted of local propaganda. At least on the radio, there were scanty reports of life in Wellen and the Security Council. Since then, he has not dared to venture out. He receives his goods from the weekly bus that stops at the edge of the woods. He became quite an alcoholic and did indeed stay to himself. He would occasionally have visitors from his past, but they too were not permitted to stay more than one night."

Maklober squinted in Lewy's direction. "How do you know all this information about Papez?"

Lewy whispered back, "It's common knowledge among journalists. I have a friend at the Wellen paper."

Maklober got up slowly to stretch his aching legs. His knee was better but still sore. He let out a small cry.

"What happened?" asked Lewy. Maklober at first hesitated, then explained his predicament, at times stopping to look out for patrols and Lewy's reaction. Lewy's eyes were fixed on Maklober as he intently listened to the story. "You actually met Moch?"

"Yeah, I've been trying to catch him for years."

Lewy now turned his attention to Papez's house. "It's getting late, let's make our way to the house," said Lewy.

"Hey, Lewy, before we go, what do you make of this flyer?" asked Maklober. Lewy sat back, and under the glowing light of the hot afternoon sun, read the notice.

He raised his eyebrows and said, "Where did you find this?"

"Along the way."

"It looks like a warning, but I can't make out the last word," said Lewy. "I remember long ago that there was an attack in the woods, but the incident was hushed up tighter than a drum. I never found out."

"Whatever it is, the villages along the river seemed to be pretty spooked by it," said Maklober.

"Well hold on to it," said Lewy. "We'll ask Papez about this if we get a chance."

By late afternoon, there was no further activity in the vicinity. They cautiously walked up to the house and looked through the window. Papez was sitting in a high-backed rocking chair reading a book. A small light illuminated the scantily-furnished room and a small fire blazed in the fireplace. A half-empty bottle of red wine stood on the side table; his second of the day. They knocked. After what seemed like an eternity, Papez opened the door. He teetered a little and slurred his words. He was bewildered to see the doctor.

"Lewy, is that you?"

"Yes, my friend."

"My God, it's been years. Come in."

"Papez, this is my friend, Maklober."

"Come in. What the hell is going on? I hear the Kitab is in an uproar."

"Let me fill you in," said Lewy.

Papez got out two glasses and poured them some wine. Lewy took about an hour to explain the whole story.

Papez sat up in his chair, nearly knocking down his glass of wine. "My God! Finally some excitement around here!"

"Can you help us?" asked Lewy.

"Any way I can. They don't watch me too closely, but they do have an eye on my general habits. I don't get too many visitors, and you are a surprise," said Papez.

"We got a glimpse of the routine today," said Lewy.

"How?"

"We hid out in the forest. We saw regular patrols come by but none approached your house," said Lewy.

"They never do. I never talk to them. At times, I peer out the window and look. They don't do much," said Papez.

"Do they come all night, too?" asked Maklober.

"No. One night, though, I happened to see a small computerized animal with a camera and a microphone outside my window. At first I thought it was the wine, as you can see that this has become my friend. The routine repeated itself night after night."

A hush fell over the room as Maklober and Lewy put down their glasses and looked at each other without uttering a word. A cold sweat broke out on their faces. "We didn't see any robot during the day," said Maklober, breaking the silence.

"Are you sure, Papez?" asked Lewy.

"Yeah, the morning patrol takes the robot back to the village and the last patrol of the day drops it off. In fact, they should be coming in a few minutes. They are fairly punctual in that regard," said Papez.

"You seem so nonchalant," said Maklober as he wiped off the sweat on his eyebrows with his sleeve and let out a deep breath.

"I'm used to it by now, but you're right. In all the excitement I forgot to warn you." With that, Papez sprang to his feet, wobbled a little, and then said, "The two of you hide out in my bedroom in the back. I'll dim the lights. After they leave, I'll close the drapes." Maklober and Lewy ducked under the windows and crawled over to the bedroom.

As they closed the door, Maklober said, "Won't they suspect something?"

Papez didn't look at them directly. Peering at them from the corner of his eye, he said, "No, from time to time, I turn off the lights and cover the windows. They've never questioned me about it."

Maklober slowly got up in agony. His knee was sore from crawling on the bare floor. He whispered as he cringed in pain, "I hope for all of our sakes you're right." Maklober and Lewy remained vigilant, trying to stay to the side of the windows.

"Can we trust him, Lewy?" asked Maklober softly.

"I'm not so sure, but to be on the safe side, let's stay out of sight of the windows and take turns tonight taking guard. I suspect he'll pass out from too much wine." They waited until Papez came in to tell them when the coast was clear. They looked at each other with weary eyes, knowing this would be a long night.

Papez prepared dinner. They were ravenous by now. All the excitement earlier had eliminated their desire to eat. Lewy and Maklober were grateful for the hospitality. They found some thick blankets and extra pillows in Papez's room, found a corner in the cabin away from the windows, and laid out the blankets on the floor. Lewy lay down first and fell fast asleep while Maklober stood guard. They took turns throughout the night awakening each other to be on the lookout.

***

Moch had already entered the Grenzen Line and was at the furthermost boundary, close to the Mahlpatrol's headquarters. He realized that he was in the vicinity and quickly traveled north, as the headquarters were in the south. He wanted to reach the waterway to make his way down to the Port of Lub. This was quite a task as it was difficult to first navigate to the entryway and then locate a craft to transport him. The entryway was located in the northern parts. Given the treacherous conditions, he would need a specially-designed vehicle. He had again reached the Grenzen Line. He waited until nightfall to cross over. Typically, the northern parts were rather barren and dotted with several huge warehouses for distribution and storage. Materials were delivered from the waterway and transported to these villages by trucks. The terrain was unsuitable for trains.

The village immediately north was quiet. The townspeople had already retired for the night. The next morning, there was a lot of commotion as the Mahlpatrol was in full force looking out for the fugitives. Also, trucks continued to transport items and materials to the rest of the Kitab. Moch stowed away on one of the trucks carrying workmen to the entryway. As usual, he observed the activity prior to taking action. He saw that the workers were unshaven, with dirty faces. He didn't understand, but didn't question it further. He found some clay and dabbed his face. He was already unshaven. Fortunately, he had gotten a crew cut prior to leaving Wellen. Everyone in the Kitab kept their hair short for uniformity. Once on board, he repositioned the Transcript, which he had hidden under his uniform.

"What are you doing?" asked one of the workers.

In a low voice, Moch said, "Just trying to get comfortable. I have a stomachache and feel bloated." The worker turned away in disgust. The ride continued in silence.

The Mahlpatrol had stopped the truck for inspection prior to entering the roadway to the high-speed route. Moch tried to keep calm and unobtrusive. Fortunately, the workers did not carry any forms of identification. He could hear the guards talking to each other. They were confident that Moch couldn't have entered this way so quickly. The waterway was in more or less a clandestine position in this part of the Kitab. They told the driver to move on. Everyone stayed huddled together in the back as the truck picked up speed and drove away.

Once the truck reached the waterway, the workers loaded the materials onto uniquely-shaped barges. The captain's bridge was located at the bow and along the expanse, there was room for storage on deck. There were two prongs that split from this main part, continuing aft ward and were also used for storage. Underneath, there was room for the workers and more supplies. The tips of the two prongs housed propellers in the event that the barge had to navigate around obstacles along the waterway. In case of attack, this was also a way to escape. The waterway was treacherous, filled with various obstacles that could potentially damage the crafts. Rocks jutted out from the shore in certain areas. Without warning, the gentle flowing waterway would turn into rapids. The ships could potentially veer off course, crashing into the bank.

The trip to the Port of Lub would now take about a day, as there were many stops along the way. Men were dropped off and picked up at small ports. They also loaded and unloaded supplies. Moch thought it was strange that the ports were located on only one side of the river.

The men were housed in simple quarters below decks. They talked among themselves, but did not know one another. They came from different villages to help prevent banding together in unity. The Mahlpatrol was stationed up on deck for riot control and security. Moch was in a rather precarious situation. His benefactors had no idea of his whereabouts, and he couldn't communicate with them to apprise them of his status. He would just have to wait it out. He stayed to himself, mingling with others and then only when absolutely necessary. He ate in the cafeteria and slept in bunks with the other men. His disguise held strong.

Though Moch had turned to a life of crime, he was quite affable. He still had remnants of his baby face, which made him appear trustworthy. This is what really enraged the Security Council. They believed in him. When not pursuing illegal activity, he let down his guard and spoke with others in a calm and relaxed way. People instantly took a liking to him. He would help the elderly with their chores. He was quite gentle around kids and pets. One day in the cafeteria, one of the workers involved him in a lively discussion over the virtues of uniformity.

"In our town," he said, "we revel in the fact that the level of production from our factories wins first place awards every year. We attribute this to our commitment to success." After a while of hearing these platitudes, several of the workers turned away in boredom.

Moch was listening intently, and then said, "What do you make?"

With that, there was a hush. Everyone looked around suspiciously. Moch waited until this fear subsided.

"What did I say?" Moch looked at the others with raised eyebrows and his mouth ajar. The worker slowly turned his head and looked over his shoulder in the direction of the door.

As there was no guard, he turned back around to face Moch and said quietly, "That information is not allowed to be shared. We would be imprisoned if news got out." One of the other workers leaned over. He had foul-smelling breath and spoke with a gruff voice. Moch tried to recoil but the man drew closer and grabbed his arm.

"By the way, where are you from, my friend? This is common knowledge in the Kitab," he said.

Moch grabbed the man's hand and firmly placed it back on his lap. He confidently said, "Forgive me. I of course know that. I guess in the excitement of everything, I wasn't thinking, and it just slipped."

The first worker sat in between the man and Moch and whispered, "Well, don't let it happen again." Moch could feel their suspicion. He stayed on guard thereafter.

***

Maklober and Lewy awoke the next morning, feeling tired from guard duty the night before. They cleaned up and put on their uniforms. Papez was already up and preparing breakfast. Maklober looked out the window.

"Don't worry. The first patrol already came and picked up the scout. You're in the clear for now," said Papez.

"That's a relief," said Maklober.

"Let's eat," said Papez.

"Breakfast looks great," said Lewy.

"Thanks, I just want to make sure you have energy for your long journey."

Maklober rested his right elbow on the table, holding a fork in his hand and pointing the tines toward Papez. "Okay, but how the hell do we get outta here?"

Papez got up, went to his desk, and pulled out a rolled-up map that was tied with a small string. "Here's what you do," he said as he unrolled the map on the table. Lewy and Maklober cleared off the dishes. "Return to the village the same way you came and take the high-speed route. This will enable you to reach your destination quicker.

"This is going to be a struggle. The Mahlpatrol knows you, Lewy," said Maklober.

"Okay, Lewy, I have a small bedsheet. Fold and wear it under your uniform to look chubbier. Also, shave your face. I have some black shoe polish to dye your hair." Papez accompanied Lewy and Maklober to the edge of the woods and wished them good luck.

Lewy said, "It was great to see you again, Papez."

As a small tear welled up in Papez's eye, he said, "Same here. You guys be careful. I wish I could come, but I'm confined to this prison." Before Papez turned around to go back inside, he said, "I yearn for the days of reporting again and the camaraderie we all shared in the past. I wish I could tell your story but instead I have nothing to write. The Kitab is not interested in my writings and censors everything." Lewy and Maklober bowed their heads in silence for a few seconds, sharing in his despair.

"By the way, Papez, what do you make of this flyer?" said Maklober.

Papez looked at the flyer and handed it back to Maklober. "I don't know—I'm so isolated. Be careful, though."

Lewy hugged his longtime friend and said, "Be well, Papez." They made their way through the myriad villages on foot, partially by train, careful to avoid the Mahlpatrol and their headquarters.

Each village was different, but the landscaping and housing were similar. They all had a central marketplace. The people dressed according to the custom particular to that village, unwavering for centuries. There was no real interest in the outside world or outsiders for that matter. Their purpose for living was rather singular. They lived and worked for each other and the greater good of the Kitab. They were permitted certain luxuries such as celebrations and alcohol as long the primary premise was upheld. Many obeyed and lived their lives in this manner. Those who did not were quickly jailed or moved to another part of the Kitab. Maklober and Lewy moved quickly throughout the villages, as they did not expect to find Moch here. They went essentially unnoticed.

In the final village prior to crossing the Grenzen Line, they came across some drunken townspeople who were celebrating the end of a long shift. They found out that these partygoers belonged to the crew who would transport goods and commodities to the northern territories. The goods would then be loaded onto the waterway barges.

Lewy and Maklober left the crowd to scout for potential routes to traverse when two rather burly and quite inebriated men came out of the local tavern. They saw Maklober and Lewy and started shouting at them; unusual for these folks given the possible ramifications. This was the last thing they needed. The Mahlpatrol would surely learn of this and swoop down on the whole region.

"Maklober," said Lewy, "let me do the talking. While I have them distracted, flank around and grab the smaller guy. I'll take care of the bigger guy—he won't be expecting it."

"Hey man," said the big guy, "aren't we good enough for you?"

Lewy said, "We just stopped in for a bite but have to leave. We live in the next village and are staying in the local inn down the street."

"That was stupid," said the smaller man, slurring his words.

"What are you talking about?" asked Lewy.

"In these parts, a man stays until the last round of drinks is served."

"Sorry if we insulted you, but we have to get ready for tomorrow," said Lewy.

"Enough talking," said the bigger guy.

"Yeah, let's have some fun with these out-of-towners," said the smaller guy.

"Hey," said Lewy, "we don't want trouble, especially from the Mahlpatrol."

"Screw them," said the drunk guys in unison.

At that moment, Maklober grabbed the little guy but suddenly froze up. As a wrestler in high school, he sustained a shoulder injury that would intermittently flare up, causing him severe pain and spasms in the neck and upper back. He was in effect paralyzed until the pain subsided; usually a few minutes. He did not have the luxury to wait now. The little guy saw what happened and seized the opportunity. He quickly subdued Maklober and threw him against the wall. Maklober writhed in pain. Meanwhile, Lewy was struggling in his attempts. The big guy knew some martial arts and tried to grab hold of Lewy, but just as he was about to place a stranglehold, Lewy darted out from under him, spun around, and delivered a swift kick to the man's midsection, felling him to the ground. He then delivered another kick to his head. The man landed hard on the ground and passed out. Lewy ultimately triumphed and reasoned that he was victorious because the guy was drunk. The little guy then staggered over, not realizing how drunk he actually was, and tried to punch Lewy in the face, and missed. By now, the adrenaline was flowing, and Lewy first ducked, then struck the little guy in the face with a swift uppercut. The man fell backwards, but caught himself against the wall. He stood tall and lunged once again at Lewy.

Maklober tried to get up to help but was in so much pain, he sat back down. "Sorry, Lewy," he said.

"No problem," said Lewy, and delivered a swift kick to the man's face. He fell like a ton of bricks.

"Not bad for an old man," said Maklober.

"Are you all right?" asked Lewy.

"Yeah, just froze up from an old wrestling injury."

He got up slowly, and the pair dragged the two men behind a dark building. A crowd was starting to form outside the bar. As they saw no further action, they went back in to continue partying. "Hey Maklober," said Lewy. "This may be our ticket to the northern territories."

"How?"

"I heard some of the townspeople in the inn say that there will be an envoy of trucks heading up north tomorrow with a large load of goods. These two will not be missed. We'll change into their clothes and leave them here in the dumpsters. In the morning, they'll be too frightened to call for help. By the time they wake up, we'll be long gone. Let's go and get back to the envoy. I saw it as we entered the village."

"Good idea," said Maklober.

***

Moch's confident plotting was broken by a thunderous crash. The boat lurched as it stopped, forcing Moch to grab the wall to catch his balance. Alarms pierced the air, and the crew was summoned to the decks.

"What the hell happened?" screamed Moch.

There was commotion everywhere. "Oh no, the Tieren are attacking the ship. It will take days to fix. On top of that, we are in a vulnerable position for future attack," said one of the men Moch had befriended earlier. Moch shuddered. The Tieren were a society of creatures that was rather secretive and elusive. No one knew the details of their organization.

As the commotion continued, he heard one of the other crewman say, "We can't row ashore and must anchor here." Moch tried to stay out of sight for fear of capture. As the room where he was hiding was now compromised, he cautiously went out and found that the adjoining room was still intact. There was no one inside, just plenty of crates. As his curiosity over the attack was piqued, he took the Transcript out from his uniform and hid it behind one of the crates, in case he was searched. Then he went back to the damaged area and saw a gaping hole on the side of the ship. There were dead bodies floating in the area. These creatures were interesting in a horrifying way. They were human in appearance, but had massive beaver-like heads and razor-sharp teeth. Why they evolved this way eluded him. It was not his concern for the moment, though. The crew had to first remove the dead bodies, which was a chore, given their weight. Some of them were pinned up against the side of the ship partially wedged in the damaged wall. What complicated matters further was that removal could let more water into the cargo areas. The captain radioed the Mahlpatrol for help. *Great,* thought Moch. *What a mess! I can't even escape because we're stranded in the middle of this waterway.*

He returned to his hiding place and ducked behind the crates. As there was no register of names to check, he wouldn't be missed, especially in this mayhem. Meanwhile, the crew was making progress in removing the bodies. The Mahlpatrol arrived with helicopters. One of the ships caught up in the traffic jam radioed to the Mahlpatrol that they were transporting building materials to the Port of Lub. The workers loaded fiberglass onto a small craft and sailed down to the ravaged ship. Using a laser, they were able to weld pieces onto the ship's side. This would be a temporary measure until they reached dry dock. Once repaired and tested for leaks, they were on their way. The Mahlpatrol stayed behind to direct traffic and provide security. For now, there were no more creatures in the vicinity. Moch was safe, at least for the moment.

CHAPTER 9

Once everything calmed down, Moch joined the group of workers he met earlier. This time, he kept his mouth shut and listened to the others. In the course of discussion, one of the workers talked a little about the Tieren. He sat hunched over on his chair, drawing everyone closer to him.

He said, "Once, about twenty years ago, my friend wanted to find out more about this society. He was young and foolish. With only a rifle and some food rations, he paddled along the waterway in a small, non-motorized craft. We never heard from him again. The Mahlpatrol found his craft torn asunder but no sign of him. He never communicated with us again. We assumed the worst and eventually gave up on rescue efforts. Since then, no one has dared to pull this stunt again."

"That was foolish," said Moch's friend.

One of the other workers chimed in, "Luckily, they've never wandered out of their territory into our towns. From overhearing some of the Mahlpatrol from time to time, I've learned that they require water regularly for survival. Additionally, the waterway consists of nutrients that may also be linked to their survival." Moch's interest was piqued, but he remained quiet. He lowered his eyebrows in contemplation.

"Why are you so quiet?" asked his friend.

"Oh, just listening. I've only heard scanty reports also and often wondered why the Superiors never sank money into further research." said Moch.

"For one, they don't have the money, and secondly, they feel that fear of the Tieren serves as a way of control."

"Weird," said Moch.

"It is, but until that happens, we have to steer clear. Fortunately, they seem to fear the Mahlpatrol and will stay away whenever they are present. This attack was probably random and a gamble on their part."

"But why do they attack? They don't seem to gain anything by it, such as goods or products."

"Purely instinctive," he said. "If they see a ship or any other structure on the waterway, they attack it. It doesn't seem to be an organized, premeditated effort. It's almost a reflex."

"So how do you prevent these attacks?" said Moch. "After all, there is a continuous stream of traffic on a daily basis."

The man paused, his brows furrowed, as he looked sideways at Moch. "We can't, at least until we know the workings of this society. For now, the Mahlpatrol has to carry a constant presence."

Moch nodded and kept quiet so he wouldn't arouse any more suspicion.

"I got to get back to my post," said the man, guardedly.

"Yeah, me too," said Moch as he lowered his eyes and scurried away. As he walked back to his hiding place, the alarms once again sounded. The loudspeaker crackled. The man on the other end shouted that two of the Tieren were still alive and had boarded the ship, but one had died in the process. The other managed to escape.

When Moch returned to his hiding place, he discovered that this part of the ship was ransacked. The Transcript was missing! He reasoned that the creatures had found it. The one who escaped probably swam off with it. He looked around the crates and through the stacks of boxes but didn't see the package. Sweat built up on his face and armpits. He doubted that anyone on board would have discovered it. There would have been too much excitement. He decided to jump ship and go ashore. He swam quickly in the turbulence created by the ship's activity and for the most part underwater. He was also an accomplished swimmer. He found a hiding place in the brush and settled down for the rest of the day. He cursed his situation as the bank of the river was muddy and cold. Once the commotion stopped, the river traffic resumed. As Moch was searching for food, he heard some rustling of leaves slightly inland and surmised at first that there were small animals scurrying about. He then saw out of the corner of his eye a squad of four Tieren policemen patrolling the area. They were making sounds to each other that were foreign to him. He could see one of the men wave his arm toward the river. Moch quickly hid and was quite scared at their sight. As he lay in the brush, the squad encircled him and each member grabbed a limb.

CHAPTER 10

"Who you?" said the head of the squad in broken English as he shrugged his shoulders trying to communicate as best as possible.

"I'm a worker who fell off one of the ships."

"Come, this way," the man said not listening to his words. Instead, he pointed his finger inland. The other members looked at each other quizzically. They couldn't understand Moch.

They led him back to the village and chained him up in one of the huts. The leader of the Tieren stopped by later that evening.

"What you want?" he asked.

"I just want to go back to my ship," said Moch.

"I no understand. Now, you stay here. I come again later. We talk again. I go now." Moch couldn't make out what they were saying. They spoke in another language to each other. At that moment, there was quite a great deal of commotion.

"What's going on?" Moch asked the guard. The guard looked at him in silence and shrugged his shoulders. When he spoke, it was in another language. He pointed with his finger or gestured with his arms. A few minutes later, Moch could see through a gap in the hut a patrolman carrying a plastic case. The Tieren had found the Transcript!

***

The next morning, Maklober and Lewy discreetly headed over to the convoy of trucks and huddled up with the other workers. As the lot comprised workers from different parts of the Kitab, everyone was a stranger. The drivers started up their trucks. The goods were already loaded. There was a separate fleet of trucks to transport the workers. The trip to the waterway took several hours. Maklober and Lewy stayed quiet and followed the lead of the others. At times, they heard murmurs but no actual conversations. At inspection points, everything went smoothly. Along the way, reports filtered in about the security efforts in progress. They heard about some attack and deployment of the Mahlpatrol to the scene and how guards were doubled at each checkpoint. No one particularly seemed to care. Maklober and Lewy were quite interested, naturally. Though craving to speak with each other, they refrained out of fear of capture. Maklober was especially worried, as the Mahlpatrol knew about Lewy. Maklober at least was an unknown entity. Fortunately, Lewy's disguise held up well. He had shaved his beard and allowed stubble to grow, cut his hair, then dyed it from gray to black. He wore some makeup from Papez to look more rugged in the face and tucked the bedsheet under his uniform. At the main dock, the workers unloaded the cargo from the trucks and onto giant pallets. Cranes then hoisted up the pallets to the ship. This was similar to the ship Moch took earlier. Lewy was fascinated by the shape and design. He never saw these ships during his student days. Further study would have to wait for later, for now he and Maklober had to sneak aboard. Typically, the crew, once having unloaded the cargo, returned to their villages. There was a separate group of sailors.

"Damn it. The sailors are wearing different uniforms," said Maklober.

"I know, we have to find some and change," said Lewy.

"But where? We have so little time," said Maklober, panting a little. They sat in silence and observed the routine for about an hour. Maklober then whispered into Lewy's ear, "How're we going to get around this one, Lewy? This is a smaller group and surely they will all know each other."

Lewy sat in silence for a few seconds looking into the distance. The workers were starting to leave the dock to go home. They had done their work loading the ship. "You're right, this will be tougher. We may have to stow away in the cargo area and hide till we land at the Port of Lub. Walking freely will not be possible. The trip should take about a day, barring any complications," said Lewy.

"It looks like they're coming out of a room in that building next to the ship," said Maklober.

"I see that."

"The coast is clear. Let's make a run for it," said Maklober.

"I don't see any guards," said Lewy as they darted in between the buildings.

"Let's stop on the side of the entryway to the room where the sailors exited." Both peered into the window and waited. "Let's go," said Maklober. When they entered, they saw a big, burly man walking toward them.

"Shit," said Lewy under his breath. Just as Maklober was about to say something, he stopped. The man was now towering over them. He smelled of laundry detergent and spoke with a gruff voice. "I thought you men already left for the ship. You'll be late and I'll get blamed for not having all the uniforms ready. Here, take these and get out there." Lewy and Maklober looked at each other in disbelief, tore off their uniforms and gave them to the man. They quickly put on the new clothes.

"Thanks," said Lewy and Maklober in unison and ran out as fast as they could. The man looked at them in disgust, shook his head, and took the uniforms back to the laundry room.

"Boy, was that close," said Maklober.

"He must be new," said Lewy as they ran to the ship and boarded.

Once aboard, they found a hiding place and camped down. The ship set sail without event. About midway, the alarms sounded. The loudspeakers blared "Tieren are in the vicinity. All available crewmen to present to the decks, armed." The ship's captain radioed the Mahlpatrol. Lewy was intrigued.

"Who or what are these Tieren?" asked Maklober.

"I have no idea. I have never heard of them either."

"It sounds formidable, though."

"Yes, indeed," said Lewy. "Do you still have that flyer, Maklober?"

"Yeah."

"Let me see it. It says, 'Beware of the Ti ….' That's it, Tieren," said Lewy.

"But still, what or who the hell are they?"

"I don't know. Nevertheless, we can't risk going out to explore. However, we do need some food."

"I'll try to slip out," said Maklober. "No one knows me, but someone may recognize you."

"You're right," said Lewy.

"I'll head to the kitchen and try to find out what all this means."

Maklober carefully made his way to the kitchen, placing his hands over his ears whenever he passed by a speaker. He didn't know the layout of the ship so he took educated guesses. From time to time he would pass crewmembers scurrying about. He tried to figure out what all the chaos was about. He asked one of the crewmembers and got some scanty information. He pretended to be illiterate from one of the back territories. Luckily, his disguise held. He eventually reached the kitchen, grabbed some rations, and snuck back to the cargo hold. Lewy was hunched down as the Mahlpatrol squad had just completed their rounds.

"Hey, Maklober, be careful," said Lewy as he climbed up to the hiding spot. "So what did you find out?"

"These Tieren are apparently a society of animals that are as cruel as they get. They attack watercraft as they navigate around these waterways. For some reason, they attack randomly."

"Why is it called a society, as if they were humans?" asked Lewy.

"No one knows. They move about in packs and appear to be organized. I couldn't find out any more, as it was too dangerous up there; Mahlpatrol and crewmen everywhere. For the moment, our situation is marginal at best."

They ate the rations and waited it out. "These alarms are deafening and are giving me a headache," said Maklober as they ate their rations and waited. By now the alarms had changed from a continuous roar to intermittent bursts of sound. After awhile, the crew silenced the alarms and order was restored.

"The Tieren have retreated," said a man on the loudspeaker.

"That's a relief," said Maklober.

"About time," said Lewy as he folded up his empty rations package and tucked it inside his uniform.

"Good idea," said Maklober, watching Lewy's actions. The ship once again picked up cruising speed.

"Lewy, did you read about these Tieren when you were a student?" asked Maklober.

"At that time, there was no literature available and no one volunteered this information. There was just an incident in the woods that was hushed up quickly. This is interesting, however. I would like to study it further, though I know this is not possible now."

The alarms started again for what felt like an eternity; then someone came on the loudspeaker and said that one of the Tieren boarded the ship. "I didn't see anyone enter the cargo hold," Maklober said, as he looked around frantically.

"It's just a matter of time before we're caught. Surely, the Mahlpatrol will canvas the entire ship now," said Lewy.

"I don't think we should wait around to find out. Let's jump overboard and take our chances," said Maklober.

"Are you crazy?" said Lewy.

"We have no choice; either be jailed in the Kitab or succumb to the Tieren," said Maklober.

"Getting caught sounds like the better of the two options," said Lewy.

"Maybe, but we can still get out of this by going along the shoreline," said Maklober.

"What about the Tieren?"

"They seem to be afraid of getting close to the Mahlpatrol and quite possibly strangers in general," said Maklober.

"This may work. But even if we did get caught, we probably could talk our way out of it," said Lewy. "I know the ambassador."

"I would rather not take that chance," said Maklober.

Lewy thought about this for awhile and eventually agreed. "The Kitab would not give us any mercy on this one. Spending the rest of our life in a Kitabian jail would be worse. At least Papez has a house, even though he's a prisoner."

They slipped down from their hiding area and found an opening in the cargo hold. The doorway was massive, but there was a smaller opening off to the side. They were above water at this point and slowly opened the door. No alarm sounded, at least for the moment. There were Mahlpatrol everywhere.

"How do we proceed?" asked Lewy.

"We'll have to swim to the shoreline," said Maklober.

They slipped into the cold, muddy water and raced to the shore underwater. It was difficult to see due to the sludge generated by all the river traffic. Fortunately they didn't have far to go, only about fifty yards. The alarm sounded on the bridge, signaling the opening of the cargo door. The Mahlpatrol watched the pair swim to shore.

"Forget them," said one of the senior officers. "The Tieren will get them for us." Everyone laughed.

Maklober and Lewy carefully concealed themselves in the foliage and waited for the ship to leave. They knew the Mahlpatrol would not enter the woods. The pair started to move downstream, keeping an eye out for the Tieren.

"This is interesting," said Lewy, "the tracks made by these creatures are quite bizarre. They almost have human qualities to them. The footprints are primate in nature. They appear to be two-legged creatures. They could very well be aborigines!"

"My understanding is that they are beaver-like, with razor sharp teeth," said Maklober.

"This may be a costume or disguise. Remember, no one has ever come close to them," said Lewy.

"Well, let's not find out," said Maklober. "Keep moving. We don't even know how far the Port of Lub is from here."

"Well, we can always try to board another ship," said Lewy.

"Don't even think about it. We have to go on foot the rest of the way," said Maklober.

They had covered quite a bit of ground along the shoreline. It was getting dark. They took cover slightly inland and saw a camp set up in a clearing. The two men quietly crawled over to the camp to inspect the layout. There were ten huts arranged in odd configurations, almost haphazardly. The front of one hut faced the side of another, and the rear faced the front of yet another hut. The common area was in the center, which seemed to be the origin of routes of travel. Though quite dark, there was what appeared to be a row of buildings in the background, which seemed to represent work areas, perhaps for manufacturing tools or other primitive devices.

"This must belong to the Tieren," said Maklober.

"We must tread very carefully."

"It looks deserted. They must be out on a mission or gathering food and supplies."

"But where are the women or the females?" asked Lewy.

"Interesting point. Perhaps they are equals in this society and participate in hunting and security," said Maklober.

"They may actually be more advanced than I thought," said Lewy.

"Yeah, this looks like a small village." Suddenly, they heard loud screams in the distance. "What the hell is that?" asked Maklober.

"I don't know, but let's hide back by the shoreline," said Lewy. They crouched down in the brush and found foliage to cover their heads, and waited and watched. The center area was now lit with torches, making it easier to observe. A large crowd of Tieren marched into the tiny village, screaming and laughing. Maklober and Lewy sat in silence, eyes intently focused on the scene in front of them. The Tieren were carrying dead rabbits. The ones who had more than one in their hands were yelling in triumph. Luckily, Maklober and Lewy were still out of view. In the midst of the screams, Lewy whispered to Maklober, "I hope our scent doesn't give us away." Maklober nodded his head in silence.

As the light grew brighter, Maklober lay prone on the soft, cool ground under the foliage. Lewy joined him. Maklober then whispered in disbelief, "Look, Lewy, they look like primates. They can stand on two legs but have beaver-like faces and razor-sharp teeth."

"This is fascinating," said Lewy.

There appeared to be quite a great deal of commotion and excitement. One of the Tieren was holding a small, collapsible plastic case. Maklober turned on his side to face Lewy. "I wonder what they found," said Maklober.

"I don't know, but it has markings from the Kitab. I see the familiar insignia," answered Lewy in a strained and excited voice.

"Wait," said Maklober, watching them open the case, as his voice slowly became louder, "that looks like the Transcript Moch stole!"

"How did they get their hands on it?" asked Lewy.

"I don't know," said Maklober, "maybe they captured Moch."

"Who knows," said Lewy, "but if we don't try to get out of here, we may suffer the same fate."

They sat up now, silently rejoicing that the Tieren hadn't heard them. Maklober stretched out his legs to relieve the ache caused by sitting for so long in a crouched position. They watched further and saw that the Tieren communicated with primitive sounds and hand gestures. Everyone seemed to know their roles and positions. The Transcript was quickly taken to one of the buildings, probably to be opened and studied. There was a hierarchy, but the men found it difficult to separate out the males from the females.

"Perhaps they are hermaphrodites," said Maklober.

"Or they have no other distinguishing secondary sex characteristics. All of them seem to be involved in the domestic chores as well as hunting and gathering," said Lewy.

The local fauna consisted of small animals, which served as the Tieren's sustenance. The flora appeared to be green plants and fruits. There was water in just about every container present.

"This must be their main form of hydration," said Lewy. "Without this, they would surely die."

The Tieren then carried out the chores of the day. *There was quite a remarkable order to their routine*, thought Lewy. One group was in charge of cleaning the village, another in the work area, and yet another group prepared the food and washed the utensils. They wore primitive skins, but were for the most part bare.

"What do we do now, Lewy?" asked Maklober.

"I think for now we just wait and observe. We can't move till later tonight, otherwise we will surely be seen. We must eventually move back to the shoreline and then on to the Port of Lub."

Maklober interjected, "But we don't even know how far that is from here! There are no watercrafts nearby. And what about the Transcript and Moch?"

Lewy whispered hurriedly, "We can't worry about Moch. He'll have to fend for himself. Once we get back to the Port, we'll alert the authorities. I think it will be too risky to get the Transcript. The hut is heavily guarded. We can't compromise out position."

At that moment, Maklober heard a rustling sound in the brush and looked back. Before he could react, two of the creatures grabbed Maklober and Lewy in strangleholds and two others tied their hand behind their backs. Maklober was so taken aback he forgot everything he learned as a wrestler. They were told to walk, and soon entered the village.

CHAPTER II

Maklober and Lewy were taken into one of the huts, made to sit down, and secured to a pole. A few minutes later, a man with graying hair and wrinkles around his eyes and face came in and looked at them for a few minutes in silence. He seemed to be the leader, based on his demeanor and the way the others treated him with deference.

"What you want? Who you?" he said in broken English, finally breaking the long and painful silence.

"We were tourists on the last boat and fell overboard during one of your attacks," said Lewy.

"Now you our prisoners," he said in both English and then in his language as he waved his arms in the air.

With that, the others cheered in jubilation.

"What do you intend to do with us?" asked Maklober.

"You wait," as he looked straight at them, shrugging his shoulders.

They languished there alone, tied to the pole, for the majority of the day, watching the Tieren carry out their chores. Lewy observed their routine carefully. They rarely communicated with each other. Every now and then one would look at the other and then carry out a task as if they were telepathic. After awhile, it seemed that they were so organized and practiced in their duties, that there was no reason to speak. They cleaned the grounds and prepared the food in silence. Lewy and Maklober didn't speak with each other, either.

At nightfall, the leader came back with two fresh guards. He towered over Maklober and Lewy, looked at them directly, and said that he was planning on using them as a bargaining chip.

He faltered somewhat on his words then said, "Superiors take our commander. They want study him. We want him back. We use you. The Superiors say yes. We meet tomorrow."

That night, they were led to another primitive dwelling and chained to the center pole. They slept on hay and were guarded by huge Tieren. The only light was from the moon shining outside.

"We can't tell them about the Transcript," whispered Maklober hoping the guard was dozing off.

"Hopefully, they won't understand it, and will keep it locked up for now. The Mahlpatrol will have to deal with it. Otherwise, they will have another bargaining chip for the future," said Lewy.

The guards did not know English, so the two couldn't pump them for any information. They all sat in silence in the dark. The guards would occasionally utter some words to each other in a language foreign to Lewy and Maklober. At about three o'clock in the morning, the two guards fell asleep. Maklober looked at Lewy in silence and communicated using his eyes. He motioned over to the guards. Lewy nodded his head in acknowledgment. Maklober fiddled with the chains shackled to his wrists. As he tried to slip his wrists through, there was a clanking noise. He stopped, held his breath, and looked at the guards. They were still sleeping. Lewy tried to hold still to keep quiet. Sweat was building on his forehead. Maklober eventually got one hand loose then stopped. One of the guards started to move but quickly returned to sleep. Maklober then worked on his other hand and freed himself. He looked at Lewy, then the guards, trying to find a key to the chains. He was unsuccessful. He slowly worked on Lewy's chains as quietly as possible. Just then one of the guards started to stir. Maklober froze and waited again. He then loosened the chains and Lewy was free. They crawled over to the door and looked outside. The coast was clear. They waited for a few minutes and escaped into the brush.

In the woods, they ran to the shoreline and tried to make their way down to the Port of Lub. They could hear shouts in the distance behind them. It was the Tieren learning of their escape. They were fugitives on the run from two groups now, the Superiors and the Tieren. It was just a matter of time before they were captured. They heard the rumble of a motor from a nearby ship. They slipped into the water and swam to the side of the boat. They spotted a ladder and grabbed hold. Alarms sounded from the boat. The Tieren were now on the shoreline. The crew fired their weapons, and Maklober hoped they were too close to the boat to be hit. The Tieren retreated.

The alarms stopped, and crewmen were looking into the darkness below. Lewy and Maklober climbed aboard the boat. "I'm sure this is not the end," said Lewy as they watched the crew come closer.

"Who are you?" asked one of the crewmen. As Maklober was about to answer, several other crewman and the captain appeared.

Lewy interjected and said, "We jumped from the last ship after the Tieren attack. I'm sure you heard about it." The captain and crew nodded. After Lewy explained their story of being caught and escaping, the crew eagerly led them inside to clean up, trying to make conversation in a collegial sort of way, sympathetic to their plight. The captain then came in a few minutes later with a stern look on his face. He held up a picture of Lewy that was circulated by the Kitabian police to all truck drivers and ship captains.

He looked at the crew, showing them the picture, saying, "They're fugitives, lock them up in one of the rooms down below." The crew didn't question his authority. No one knew who Maklober was and they didn't care. Lewy and Maklober looked at each other in silence. They dared not speak, given the captain's serious tone. Two of the crewman grabbed hold of them and led them down below. They tried to wiggle out but couldn't break the hold. They were thrown into a room with a small light bulb secured behind a metal grate in the upper corner and a little sliding opaque door within the door for someone on the outside to look inside. There were two small cots on either wall.

Once in the lockup, Maklober spoke in a soft voice, "Well, this is a much better fate at least. I dare not think what the Tieren would have done to us."

Lewy nodded his slowly and said, "You're right. For now, we may have saved the Superiors from handing over the leader."

Maklober furrowed his eyebrows. "Or there may be an all-out war between the two societies. I shudder to think."

Lewy went on to say, "We were their bargaining chip. The caught leader must be a top figure in their organization. He would certainly not only serve as political and economic help but also scientific. I would love to be part of that study, personally speaking."

"Yeah, well, Lewy," said Maklober, "for now we may also be part of a study if we don't figure a way out of this one." Both men then lay down on the cots and fell fast asleep as the fatigue of the past day quickly caught up with them.

CHAPTER 12

The ship landed at the Port of Lub uneventfully. Lewy and Maklober were escorted to the authorities. Once on dock, the Mahlpatrol questioned the pair, but at this point they were more interested in what the men had found out about the Tieren. They knew that they didn't have the Transcript and surmised that it was lost. Lewy explained his observations in great detail, so much so that it took about an hour, all told. The news was captured on tape for archival purposes. Off the record, he told them that the Tieren had the Transcript. This was met with great disappointment and grave concern.

The authorities asked them about Moch, but Maklober and Lewy didn't have any knowledge of his whereabouts. They were taken into custody. At headquarters at the Port of Lub, they were interrogated.

"Lewy, this was quite foolish of you," said one of the Mahlpatrol members.

"I know. I just wanted to find Moch and clear my name."

"What do you know of the Transcript?"

"Just that the Tieren found the case. We don't know their intentions. I doubt they would know its meaning."

"Let's hope so," said the Mahlpatrol.

Maklober was led into another room. He sat for awhile, watching the bare stone walls, looking for something to break up the endless gray. There was nothing. A guard entered, breaking the cold silence.

"Who are you?" asked the guard.

"I'm Detective Maklober from Wellen. I came to search for Moch."

"Why didn't you contact us through diplomatic channels?"

Maklober sat on a hard chair, thinking how to answer. He looked down for a few minutes. The guard sat on the other side of a long, metal table staring intently at him. Maklober then spoke sheepishly. "I was so embarrassed that Moch escaped again. I just wanted to find him myself."

The guard stood up and said, "That was stupid, nevertheless. You have violated our laws and for now will have to remain in custody until we speak with the Superiors."

Maklober remained sitting and said quietly, "I understand." He was led to a jail cell. He saw other prisoners but was relieved to see that he didn't have any roommates. Soon, Captain Krom arrived and spoke with Maklober.

"What happens to us now?" asked Maklober.

"That will be up to the Superiors," said Krom.

When the Superiors arrived, they spoke with Lewy first. Initially, they wanted to either imprison him or let him go, but later they decided to exploit his help in studying the Tieren leader. The chief superior, known as Keph, was flanked on either side by his aides when they entered Lewy's cell. He was quite an imposing man, with graying hair. At first, no one spoke. Lewy tried to apologize but they silenced him.

After awhile, Keph said, "Doctor, we are aware of your reputation in Wellen, and your good nature, but this time you have overstepped your boundaries. What you did was foolish, careless, and as a result you nearly got yourself killed."

"But ..." said Lewy.

"Let me finish!" shouted Keph. "Additionally, the Tieren are up in arms. Our cities will have to be on extra alert until we have come to a decision regarding their leader. They have our Transcript, which we need to run our government. Do you realize what a mess this is?"

After careful deliberation, Lewy said, "I have an idea."

Chapter 13

"The Tieren are a primitive society and just want their commander back," Lewy said. "We of course want to find out more about them not only for academic interests but as a measure of protecting your cities. The Security Council will of course be very interested. We also need to retrieve the Transcript."

"Yeah, so what's your point?" said Keph.

"In truth, we will never get anything out of this commander with modern interrogation and torture techniques."

"Don't be too sure," said Keph.

"Realistically, you will not learn as much as you could. Sure, you could kill him and perform an autopsy, which would please me to no end, but you won't gain anything further, at least not at this point, anyway."

"What are you proposing?"

"I say that we implant a computer chip into his brain which will enable us to record his thoughts and also serve as a microphone and a camera to observe his society. He won't know that it has been implanted."

"How do you expect us to do this without anyone finding out?" said Keph.

"A very good friend of mine is a neurosurgeon at Sci Tech University. In conjunction with an ophthalmologist, he has done this on an experimental basis in his lab. He has just about perfected the implant in primates and begun work on a few humans. The latter were prisoners. The judicial system wanted to study the dynamics of prison life in order to more effectively guard the prisoners.

"In our society, prisoners who have committed heinous crimes have lost all rights and can be subjected to human experimentation or face the death penalty. Of course, our means are not barbaric, but do conform to legitimate scientific rules. There is a board of scientists who attest to the ethical and moral basis."

"Whatever," said Keph.

"The engineering department has also created a second-generation chip that has been proven to be quite successful in this regard."

"But how do you know this will work?"

"I can only base this upon those clinical trials. Furthermore, we must tell the Tieren that we are returning their commander unharmed."

"They will be naturally curious as to the reason," said Keph.

"We will tell them that we are fearful of their attacks on our ships and that this will be a goodwill measure to achieve harmony. They may just believe it."

"Won't they check him out and find the incision?"

"No, that's the beauty of this surgery. The wound is well-concealed with a skin graft, covered by hair. Plastic surgeons taught my friend the technique. He requested this as he had planned to return his primate subjects back to their habitat. He wanted them to look as natural as before. Thus far, it has been successful. On the human subjects, this has also fared well. We'll have to make some adjustments in this case given the rather large size and unusual shape of their heads."

"How long does the entire procedure take, including recovery time?"

"About two to three days."

"That's all?"

"Yeah."

"Go on," said Keph, thoughtfully.

"Why don't we tell the Tieren that we are considering our options for now and will get back to them in a few days?" asked Lewy.

"All we know is that they are extremely angry over losing you and Maklober as bargaining chips and may strike at will. We think that by holding their commander we can prevent any rash decisions. I will speak with their acting commander in the morning and convey our intentions. If they agree, call your neurosurgeon friend. I will want to talk to him first and will also get our own scientists on board."

"Agreed," said Lewy. "But please keep in mind that this is a very delicate issue from our standpoint as well, as vital scientific information will be shared with your society. I will have to clear it along political lines."

"Do what you have to, for your lives are on the line!"

Lewy was worried. The commander agreed, but it was far from over.

***

Later that day, Lewy spoke with Joseph. He first apologized and then filled him in on the developments. Joseph got back to him later that evening and reluctantly agreed to the plan.

"Lewy," said Joseph, sounding exasperated, "you have really gotten us all into a sticky situation. We have no business with the affairs of the Kitab, and especially with these so-called Tieren. This will violate our national security laws and place us in a compromising position. They will now know of our studies in human control and may use it against us in the future."

"I know," said Lewy, calmly. "I would appreciate your help on this one, Joseph."

"You do realize, Lewy, that our government may not comply and consider you and Maklober dispensable?"

"That's true," said Lewy. "But keep in mind that this is also our chance to learn more about this Tieren society, and as an ulterior motive, the entire Kitab region. The Superiors may in some way also be grateful if we help them to retrieve the Transcript."

"I hadn't thought of it that way," said Joseph.

"Just let the Security Council know about the plan in these terms. I am certain that they will agree."

***

The neurosurgeon and ophthalmologist were on standby, as were the operating room staff and computer crew. Joseph cleared the operation with the government and various security agencies.

The next morning, the chief superior and his aides drove to the edge of the river and met with the acting Tieren commander at a pre-arranged site. One of Keph's aides as a summer project in college studied the Tieren language. The Mahlpatrol had captured one of the Tieren during an attack on a ship. He stayed in lockup that summer but was eventually released as the Superiors didn't have any way of communicating with him. They simply took him on a ship and threw him in the river. He swam back to shore. There was no word thereafter. In the process, the aide picked up parts of the language.

Once seated, Keph said with the assistance of his aide, "We have come to offer you a proposal. We know that you are angry about losing your prisoners as we are that they have trespassed on our land. They come from the outside, a land known as Wellen."

"I never hear of this land," said the acting commander, his head held high as he peered down his long nose at Keph trying to speak in broken English. At times, he would shift to his language and the aide would translate.

Keph shifted in his chair. "It does not matter. What is important is that we want them to be imprisoned. To be fair, we will return your commander unharmed."

"What you want back?" asked the Tieren.

"We only ask that you keep to yourselves and not attack our cities or ships. Provided that you and your commander agree, we will arrange for transfer in a few days. Is that acceptable for the moment?"

"Yes." When he saw Keph about to speak, he added, "I get back later. I speak to my people. How we know our commander safe?" said the Tieren.

"I will arrange a meeting with him and one of your healers prior to the transfer."

"Yes."

There was no mention of the Transcript during the meeting. The acting Tieren commander sent word later that day consenting to the plan. The commander also responded in the affirmative, provided that the conditions were met.

***

Joseph and the surgical staff flew to the Kitab that night under a cloak of secrecy. Lewy was delighted to see his old friends again and started to prepare the labs and operating room for surgery.

Lewy went to visit Maklober at the prison that night. He could not offer much details as the guards were within earshot. Nevertheless, Lewy told him that for the moment he was safe.

"What is the general plan?" asked Maklober.

"For now, we are attempting to return the Tieren leader along diplomatic lines."

"That's crazy," said Maklober. "That won't accomplish anything. The Tieren will have more resolve to attack. We will certainly be doomed."

"Don't worry. I have an idea that might just work," said Lewy. He then went on to fill Maklober in as best as he could. In between the explanation, Lewy looked in the direction of the station to see if the guards were listening. After a few minutes, one of the guards had walked over to them and told him to hurry up as visiting time was almost over.

"That was close," said Maklober. Lewy waited till he left, then finished explaining his plan.

"I hope this works," said Maklober, "it sounds like a good plan."

"They will let you go once the plan is in motion," said Lewy. "I will stay behind to offer scientific help. If anything, it's my butt on the line."

CHAPTER 14

The Kitabian scientists were in awe of the technologic aspects of the operation. Their society was primitive in comparison. First, the computer staff set up the lab. They needed generators to handle the energy requirements of their equipment. The chip was placed in a secure position. As this was classified information, they did not explain the salient details. The scientists probably would not understand it anyway. Next, the surgeon assembled his team and prepared the operating room to Wellen standards.

Though doctors in the Kitab were theoretically quite sound and competent, financial concerns limited their abilities to provide quality care. Everyone was covered through a universal health plan, but only basic services could be offered. Surgery was limited to a few, and only then in emergency cases. Elective cases were deferred as long as possible. Over time, the people developed an attitude of futility, especially as they grew older. They knew that certain services would not be offered. Research was focused on looking for ways of saving money and proving that certain medications or procedures were not altogether that beneficial. Social services and home therapy were also limited, due to the resources required. The elderly lived with their children for as long as possible. The government provided the families a small pension to help offset the costs. Those who needed more care were eventually transferred to large nursing facilities that had little help and few resources. The mantra was to simply maintain oneself for as long as possible in the most economical way.

The surgeons and the operating room crew were quite shocked to learn of this philosophy of life and the primitiveness of the hospital facilities. In Wellen, technological advances were applauded. The inhabitants would certainly not put up with the Kitabian philosophy. Although most people in Wellen were reluctant to pay extra for medical services, they certainly demanded it. As the financial picture was bleak in the Kitab, the Superiors maintained that these technological advances, though impressive and potentially lifesaving, were just too costly to justify devoting a part of an already strained budget to these endeavors. They used this argument to alter the psyche of the people. Furthermore, the inhabitants could not afford any further tax increases. Unlike in Wellen, there was no steady stream of private donations to supplement governmental grants.

Prior to proceeding, the scientists held a conference to discuss the techniques and means of studying the Tieren society. The computer staff started. The audience was limited to the Superiors and select scientists. There was no press or lay public invited.

The first to speak was a man named Seth. He had a slight build with horn-rimmed glasses and tousled, blond hair. He studied at one of the prestigious computer colleges in Australia and was by all accounts a genius. He neither smoked nor drank. He never married and lived for his work. "First of all," said Seth, "the chip carries sophisticated circuitry to monitor the thoughts and actions of the individual. I would be happy to explain this to the scientists later, if desired. Secondly, there is a built-in camera and microphone, which will enable us to pick up conversations and visualize the workings of the society."

"This is quite incredible," said Keph, "how do you know this will work?"

"We have studied it in both humans and primates."

"In humans?" said Keph guardedly.

"Yes," said Seth. "I brought along a video demonstration of both sets of subjects. In the primates, we can appreciate some thoughts but only as rudimentary phonemes. We can pick up actions more clearly and more importantly through the interaction with their society.

"In the human population, you can see firsthand thoughts as the subject generates them. We have filtered out all the superfluous ones and only concentrated on those pertinent to our study. We can also pick up conversations and any criminal behavior in the prison."

"That is quite impressive," said the chief superior. "Not that it is any of my concern, but isn't this an invasion of privacy?"

"Definitely," said Seth. "Be assured, though, that the chip only lasts for about a year before it degenerates. We don't have the technology to keep it in any longer."

The surgeon explained the preparation of the patient and then some basic neuroanatomic principles. He prefaced his talk by explaining the technical difficulties, as he had never worked on such specimens.

"The chip will be implanted over the left cerebral cortex and it will record sensory input, language, memory, and motor abilities. A built-in microphone will pick up sounds, which can then be filtered and broken down into individual components. The visual part is trickier and is linked with a microscopic camera chip that is implanted into the cornea. With computer assistance, we can record activities occurring in the subject's environment."

The ophthalmologist was then introduced and discussed the technical aspects of implanting the camera.

The next day, the Tieren commander was brought into a conference room under the pretense of further negotiations.

He spoke in broken English and was difficult to understand. From what little fragment of recognizable words they could recognize, it sounded like he wanted to know the plan. Keph then said, "This is quite a dilemma for us."

"I help you, no?" said the commander.

"I know," said Keph. "I appreciate your patience, but we just need more assurances."

"I no understand."

"This is what we're still ironing out," said Keph. The aide had tried to his best to translate, albeit unsuccessfully.

"I no understand," said the commander, sighing.

Keph was stalling and the commander knew it. There was a momentary silence in the room. The frustration was evident on everyone's face. Just as the commander was about to break the silence, he was restrained by one of the guards and subdued with a mild sedative. He quickly went off to sleep.

"About time," said Keph. "I couldn't hang on any longer."

The surgical staff took the commander to the operating room and prepped him for surgery. The surgeons entered with their team, which consisted of a scrub nurse, an assistant, and Seth the computer engineer. The team quickly went to work. They prepped the scalp and then drilled small holes through the skull. Once they exposed the brain, the scrub nurse took the chip out of its protective housing. The chip resembled a convex plate with circuitry imbedded within. It was designed to fit over the surface of the brain. The details were classified. The Kitab members did not ask questions. Keph sat in the outer room watching the procedure on closed-circuit TV.

He said to his aide, "Perhaps we can steal this chip technology and use it as a means of leverage. Wellen will not allow us to function independently now because we have their secret."

"Don't worry, Chief," said one of the aides, "I photographed the chip last night. One of their guards didn't know of our other entrance into the safe."

"I hope you didn't cause a malfunction," said Keph.

"No, I replaced the chip and its housing components back exactly."

"Good," said Keph. "At the very least, we can use this technology on our own people to monitor their loyalty."

"Make sure our scientists observe the operation very carefully."

"It's all on camera, boss."

The surgery proceeded uneventfully. The surgeon sutured the wound and applied a skin graft. Prior to closing, Seth tested the chip. "All is operational," he said.

The leader was taken to the recovery room and then to his quarters. He would sleep for the next twelve hours.

During this time, there was a flurry of activity. Keph's staff made arrangements to transfer the leader and prepare for the healer to inspect him. Seth was busy setting up the computer lab. Lewy oversaw this part of the operation.

When the leader awoke, he was somewhat bewildered and still groggy. Keph and the surgical team assured him that all was well. They removed the bandage uneventfully.

"My God," said the others, "the incision is invisible."

"Great job!" said Keph and Lewy.

With that, Joseph, the surgeons, and the operating room staff flew back to Wellen. Lewy thanked his longtime friends for all their help. The leader then awoke and slowly regained his bearings.

"What, where?" cried out the leader.

"I am sorry to report," said Keph, "you fainted in the conference room. We did not run any tests, as this would invade your privacy."

The commander then stood up now, fully awake. He pounded his fist on the table and started yelling in his own language. Additional guards came in the room, but he stayed in place. A few English words came out in between his ranting. He agreed that testing would invade his privacy. After a few minutes, he calmed down and returned to his seat. The guards went back outside and stood by the door. The commander then pointed to the ceiling and said, "Sun or moon?"

"It's evening," said Keph. "When you first awoke, you were so agitated that we kept you sedated. We trust that you feel back to normal now."

The Tieren leader grunted.

"We plan to complete the arrangements by tomorrow. Your society has set up the site and time." Lewy and Keph left him to rest in his room. The leader could do nothing but wait now. He got up and bathed. Nothing seemed amiss, at least for the moment.

"Lewy," said Keph, "can we try out this gadget while he is here?"

"Actually, we have been all along. Let's go over to the computer lab and see the results."

They spoke with Seth. He said that so far the chip was operating well.

"What can you record?" asked Keph.

"While he was under sedation, we only recorded sleep waves and fragments of dreams. When he awoke, we could detect thoughts. I think from being locked up here, he learned some English, but we had to translate the rest," said Seth.

"How did you manage that?" said Keph.

"That's the beauty of this technology. We're able to break down the individual sounds into components, compare them to known language sounds, and then devise an alphabet. From that, we can translate into our language. With the primates, this was not possible. Your aide has also been quite helpful," said Seth.

"What has he thought so far?"

"He queried his location and surroundings. His memory of his stay here was recorded, but not any long-term registration yet. We hope to record some of his memories as a Tieren leader. Additionally, we have erased his recollection of his faint and the first post-operative day. As far as he is concerned, nothing happened."

"That's marvelous," said Keph.

"Also," Seth went on to say, "we can hear voices and natural sounds in his vicinity and see as he sees."

"Amazing," said Keph.

"It truly is," said Seth. "Our neuropsychologist in Wellen helped us with the interpretation of thoughts and memories in general. This has not yet been perfected, given the complexity. We only have rudimentary data. In the next month, or perhaps sooner, we will have the necessary software to accurately pinpoint these functions. We can then easily program that software directly into the chip from here. We don't need to perform any further surgery."

"That's good, because we won't have this chance again," said Keph.

"How long would you like to monitor him?" asked Lewy.

"I would say about three months, but as I mentioned previously, the chip can function for about twelve months," said Seth. "That will be a good window of time to collect our data, provided it is okay with our hosts."

"For now," said Keph, "let's just take it one day at a time. I want to make sure this contraption really works." Everyone agreed.

CHAPTER 15

The meeting was set up to arrange for the transfer of the Tieren commander. The Tieren healer had performed his examination and felt that all was in order. He inspected the leader for any stray marks or wounds. The graft held well and could deceive even the most practiced eye. Keph and the Mahlpatrol waited on one end of the bridge to the woods where the Tieren lived. The acting leader and some of his aides waited at the other end. The plan was to let the leader go with the understanding that they wouldn't attack the Kitab's cities or ships. The leader agreed to hold up his end of the bargain but also warned that if anyone tried to do any harm to the Tieren, they would attack. Everyone agreed. There was no hint that anything was out of order.

The Kitab crew went swiftly back to the lab to monitor the leader. "Well, Seth, what do you have for us?" asked Keph.

Seth sat in a small room in front of his computer. The room was decorated with a wall hanging depicting the Kitabian insignia and a famous former leader. There was no carpeting on the floor, just tile. Seth was in his element. He turned around with a smile on his face. He said, "So far, everything seems to be in order. Our software to translate their language is understandable. The have already checked out the commander for any injury or harm and seem satisfied. Now they are assembling in a meeting room. Let's see."

What appeared was a small room in one of the buildings that Lewy and Maklober had seen earlier. This was a primitive setting with a weathered wooden table and a few creaky chairs. The leader sat at the head of the table flanked by two assistants and what looked like two other members. The acting leader started by saying in their own language how relieved they were that the commander had returned.

"Did they do anything to you, any harm or torture?"

"No, they tried to interrogate me but failed."

"What did you see while you were there?"

"Unfortunately, not much. I was locked up in a single building. I couldn't make out any of their operations."

What followed was administrative talk. The domestic aspects were covered rather quickly. The discussion then turned to the Transcript. Keph was now glued to the monitor. The commander was especially interested.

The acting leader said in his language, "One of our crew found this plastic case in the ship after one of our attacks."

"What is it?" asked the commander.

"We don't know. There's some writing on the side and a concealed zipper. We opened it up and looked inside. There were several wires and circuitry with two keys. There was also this small disk attached to it."

"This is the software and CD required to run our government," said Keph.

"What should we do with it?" asked the acting leader.

"For now, nothing. Zip it back up," said the commander.

"That good-for-nothing prisoner isn't any help either," said the acting leader.

"Has he said anything?" asked the commander.

"No." The acting leader explained the capture and the escape of Lewy and Maklober.

"Did we learn anything from them?" asked the commander.

"No, we didn't have enough time," replied the acting leader.

The commander's face fell in disgust and then said, "I'll talk to the prisoner later. Has he tried to escape?"

The acting leader sat straight and said firmly, "No, this time we doubled the guard outside."

The commander got up and barked, "Let's make sure this time."

Seth did not know what to make of this, for there was never any mention of a prisoner previously.

"Maybe it's Moch," said Lewy.

"Oh well," said Keph, "the Tieren will take care of him for us."

"I bet the Kitab is angry for losing it," said the commander. "Interestingly, this was not part of our negotiations."

"I'm sure they're up to something," said the second in command.

"Well, it may be nothing either; just components that by themselves are meaningless. Maybe they can make another one if they had to," said the commander.

"Possibly," said one of the others.

"This is not true," said Keph. "It takes a year to produce the Transcript, given all the updates that have to be added to the software. It is no small feat. We definitely need it back."

"For the moment, it seems like they are just going to hold on to it," said Lewy.

"We'll keep monitoring them," said Seth.

The meeting ended and the commander went to his quarters for lunch and to lie down. He wondered what the plan would be now, especially since the Kitab now knew of his society. He drifted off to sleep. He dreamt about his childhood. His parents told him bits and pieces about how their society evolved. No more could be garnered by Seth.

Over the next few days, Seth monitored the daily routine. There was nothing extraordinary about these people. They were not particularly intelligent. They were primarily hunters and gatherers and required water to survive. No one really knew how their species evolved. They attacked the ships on the waterway only when their supplies were low. This would explain the random nature. For the most part, they kept to themselves. It was true that they were hermaphroditic. They must have evolved this way to perpetuate the species. They all participated in the chores. For recreation, they usually swam in the rivers or held wrestling matches. It didn't look like they were advanced enough to make alcohol or drugs. If anything, they were a rather pure and clean society. They fought when necessary.

"This is all useful information," said Keph.

Lewy was a little concerned that the Kitab would take advantage of these people and quite possibly even enslave them for their own purposes.

"What do you plan to do with this knowledge?" asked Lewy.

"For now, nothing; don't worry," said Keph. "We are going to leave them at peace. We just want our Transcript back."

"How are you going to get it?"

"We will send two of our most elite Mahlpatrol officers in to retrieve it."

"The Tieren will surely know," said Lewy.

"What I plan to do is to substitute it with a fake. They will never know the difference," said Keph.

"Clever," said Lewy.

"We have to wait for the right time, though. With Seth's help, we will know when that time occurs."

CHAPTER 16

Captain Krom and his elite squad prepared for the mission. Several years ago, Krom was instrumental in fighting off an attack from the Tierens.

Seth continued to monitor the Tierens' activities.

"They have resumed their usual lifestyle. I feel that you can now go in and try to retrieve the Transcript. They have hidden it in one of their buildings with round-the-clock guards. For now, they aren't planning to study it further."

"Is there any routine to the timings of the guards?" asked Keph.

"It seems like they have two guards all the time, except during the late morning hours. They probably figure that no one in their right mind will attack at this time of day."

"They are probably right," said Keph.

"During the middle of the night," Seth went on to say, "they have two guards who patrol the grounds. There is perhaps a three minute window of time when they lose sight of the entrance to the building. This would be your only chance. The other possibilities would be either to create a diversion, which would be messy, or subdue the guards."

"My only concern with the latter is that they will remember the attack and retaliate," said Keph.

"Okay, then you will have to go with this option," said Seth.

Krom decided to take only one other man from his elite squad within the Mahlpatrol. They formulated their plan and left the next night. This was fortuitous as it started to rain.

"This will provide adequate cover," said Krom.

They had to swim across, as the bridge was well guarded. Once ashore, they took off their wetsuits and hid them in a sack underwater. They then went swiftly and quietly to the camp.

"Everyone is inside, as we expected," said the assistant to Krom.

"This is indeed helpful," said Krom.

They watched and waited for awhile. They monitored the guards' activities and calculated their rounds to the nearest second. It was about 2 AM when they decided to make their move.

"You take the outer side," said Krom. "I'll meet you at the guard post."

Seth had given them detailed illustrations of the building, its layout, security, and entrance. They used a small portable laser to open the door. With this technology, there would only be microscopic marks on the door. No one would be able to detect it using the naked eye. Once inside, they could relax somewhat as the guards never went in. They only checked the door periodically. They found a pile of palm tree leaves sitting in the corner of the room. Excitedly, the assistant went over to search.

"Sir," said the assistant, "there are just palm tree leaves here. Where's the Transcript? It's missing."

***

At headquarters, Keph and the others were waiting.

"The Transcript is missing." said Krom.

"What!" said Keph.

"There was only a pile of palm tree leaves in the room," said the assistant.

"They must have moved it," said Keph.

"Why? Did they know about our plans?" asked Krom.

"I don't think so. We kept this mission top secret. Furthermore, they haven't taken any action yet," said Keph. "Seth, any ideas?"

"So far, I don't see any activity. Are you sure it wasn't anywhere else in the room?"

"Positive! We stayed as long as possible but had to get out of there. Time was running out."

"Okay, I'll keep monitoring their movements," said Seth.

"Let us know the instant you find out," said Keph.

"This is indeed terrible news," said Lewy.

***

The next morning, everyone assembled in the computer room. Lewy was escorted in by his guard. Seth had been up all night. He was typing away at the computer, adjusting the monitor and working on translating the conversations. He got up, stretched, and yawned. He went over and poured himself another cup of coffee, his third since the previous night. He then sat back down and directed everyone to the monitor. The Tieren leader met privately with his second in command who had been the acting leader.

"I was thinking about this case. I think it holds quite a great deal of significance to the Kitabians. They don't want us to know that and have kept it quiet. They probably figured that we wouldn't know what to do with it anyway."

"They may be right," said the second in command. "What do we do with it now?"

"Nothing for the moment. Let's keep it as bargaining chip for the future. We have to guard it well. They may try to come and get it. In the meantime, call our head toolmaker. Maybe he can make some sense out of it."

"Will do."

"I hope they don't destroy it in the process," said Keph.

***

The toolmaker and second in command arrived in seconds to the commander's residence. They watched while the toolmaker slowly unzipped the case and looked inside. There were several wires and a hard drive for the disk enclosed.

"I have no idea what this could be. It looks like something from outer space."

"Well, just be careful with it," said the Commander.

"There's this piece of plastic on the machine that looks like it may move up and down and two small pieces of metal attached," said the toolmaker.

"The plastic is a switch and the pieces of metal are keys that are meant for security purposes. We aren't allowed to possess both keys simultaneously," said Keph, still glued to the monitor.

"There's also this wire with prongs at the end," said the toolmaker.

"Let's not break it," said the acting leader.

With that, they zipped it back up and returned to the leader. "We can't make any sense of it," said the toolmaker.

"What should we do with it?" asked the second in command.

"I think it will now be too dangerous to keep it here. The Kitabians will definitely attempt to get it back," said the commander. They covered up the case in a large palm tree leaf and headed out to another hiding place.

***

"What are their plans?" asked Lewy.

"I don't know, but they seem interested," said Keph. "They know it carries some importance."

"Like what?"

"I'm not at liberty to say. It won't have any meaning to these creatures, though."

They watched as the commander assembled a security crew and selected two of its top members to take the Transcript to a secret place.

"I'm sorry, gentleman," said Seth. "As the commander is not planning on going, I won't be able to follow them, unless of course we can attach a tracking device."

"No such luck," said Keph.

The room was quiet, until Keph suddenly spoke in his well-known baritone voice.

"Okay," he said. "Krom, I need you to shadow them."

"We'll be ready in an hour," said Krom.

With that, Krom and his assistant left to pack their gear.

***

"This will be tough," said the assistant. "We'll be following them in broad daylight and then on their turf."

"I know," said Krom. "I have an idea, though. Since our helicopters fly regular patrols over the Kitab and Tieren areas, they can track the journey. We'll hitch a ride with one of the ships on the waterway for as long as we can."

"That's a good idea," said the assistant. Keph agreed.

Arrangements were made. The most experienced of the pilots flew the helicopter. The pilot spoke personally with Keph and Krom. He went on to say, "The Tieren may be on to us, so I will just follow the routine flight plan. We have radar and can track their movements, though."

"That will be great," said Krom.

"I'll keep in radio contact with you," said the pilot.

***

Lewy stayed behind to monitor the commander's actions, at least for the moment. He spoke with Maklober that evening in the jailhouse.

"What's going on?" asked Maklober.

"For now, the Transcript is in the Tieren's hands."

"Any sign of Moch?"

"No, he must have either drowned or is on his way back to Wellen. There was some talk that the Tieren captured him and are holding him prisoner. The Mahlpatrol has sent a team to track down the Transcript," said Lewy.

"I gotta get out of here to find Moch," said Maklober. "He would still have the Transcript, if anyone does."

"They will catch you again," said Lewy.

"Don't worry; they're preoccupied with the Transcript and have forgotten about Moch. Can you help me?"

"Any way I can," said Lewy.

After careful and quiet deliberation, they devised a plan. Periodically, they spoke louder about general information so as to not arouse suspicion.

"What are you going to do?" asked Maklober.

"I plan to stay behind and help Seth."

Just then, one of the guards walked by. He looked at them suspiciously. Both waved. He moved on in disgust.

"Okay. Maklober," said Lewy. "I'll visit again."

Later that night, Lewy came back to the lock up and saw one of the guards get up and go out, leaving the other guard to watch the prisoner. Once the first guard had left and closed the door, Lewy snuck back from Maklober's cell and grabbed the guard's head and neck from behind until he slumped to the ground unconscious. Lewy felt the man's neck for a pulse, and when satisfied he was still alive, went back to free Maklober then quickly returned to his room.

Before leaving he said, "Good luck."

CHAPTER 17

Krom and his assistant made their way to the dock and boarded the ship to the Northern Territories. The helicopter took off on its routine patrol. The Tieren were coursing through the woods.

Moch was still in captivity. He heard the helicopter and reasoned that the Kitabians were coming for the Transcript. In the flurry of activity, the guards outside of Moch's hut came in to tell the other guard that they had to join the others and that he would now be solely responsible. Moch knew his opportunity had arrived. He swiftly overtook the lone guard and escaped. He followed the trail of the guards.

***

Krom and his assistant were following the Tieren by both radio and ship. The helicopter pilot notified them of the location. Krom and his assistant asked the captain to gradually slow down. They slipped off the boat and swam to shore, hiding their wet suits in a waterproof container underwater. They crawled over to the location and hid in the dense underbrush. To their amazement, they saw the Tieren carry the Transcript to a new hiding place, a cave with two guards at the entrance. They stayed back to avoid capture. "Let's set up camp here," said Krom.

***

Moch reached the cave and scouted out the layout. Earlier, he saw Krom and his assistant from the corner of his eye in the distance. As they had not moved, he plotted out his plan. He snuck up to the cave and grabbed hold of one of the guards. He let out a yell and the other guard ran over. "Who the hell is that?" said Krom to his assistant as they lay hiding in the brush.

"I don't know," he replied. Moch had killed the guard he was holding swiftly by snapping his neck. He then turned his attention to the other guard, who was holding a spear directed right at him. "Who you?" he asked in broken English.

"I've been commissioned from the Mahlpatrol to take back our property you stole." Using his martial arts training, Moch ducked underneath the thrust spear, spun around, and delivered a hard kick to the Tieren's midsection. The guard fell to the ground in agony. He was writhing in pain and unable to get up. Moch dropped to the ground and proudly stated, "I'm from the Mahlpatrol."

Krom heard him and turned to his assistant, squinted, and said, "Shit, now they think it's us." The guard was in too much pain to notice that Moch wasn't wearing the Kitabian insignia. Moch hid by the side of the cave for a few seconds. More guards rushed out and saw their fallen comrades. The first one was dead and the second still alive but in great agony. He was able to tell them it was the Mahlpatrol, the only word he could understand. They then set out to comb the area.

CHAPTER 18

Moch capitalized on the opportunity and snuck inside. He found that there were three entrances. He arbitrarily chose one, which set off an alarm. The Tieren toolmaker laid a fine piece of twine on the ground that when tripped, triggered a mallet on the wall to strike a drum several times. He ran through anyway and saw the Transcript locked up in a cage in a corner of the big room. Unsure how to get it, he went back to the entrance. At that moment, a guard jumped out and tried to grab hold of Moch. The guard turned out to be a formidable opponent. Moch tried to subdue him with his kickboxing skills, but the guard was able to defend himself. "You're pretty good," said Moch. The guard looked at him blankly, unable to understand the language. Moch and the guard were entangled in hand-to-hand combat. The guard managed to pin Moch against the wall of the cave, pressing his large hand against his face. Moch was about to succumb, but then remembered a move from his training days. He grabbed the guard's elbow and squeezed over the ulnar nerve as hard as he could. This led to severe tingling and pain. The guard let go and tried to grab Moch with his other hand. Moch was too quick and delivered a thunderous punch to his face. The guard fell back and Moch pounced on him. They both landed on the ground. This time, Moch prevailed. He snapped the guard's neck, quickly killing him. He searched the dead guard's pockets, found the key, and then returned to open the cage. He took the Transcript and made his way back to the shoreline.

***

Krom and his aide looked up to see themselves surrounded by Tieren. They were taken to the cave in chains. Once they arrived, the Tieren and the prisoners learned that the Transcript was missing. "Where box?" asked one of the Tieren guards.

"It wasn't one of us," said Krom, as he pleaded with them to let him call his boss so that they could double the guards. "He's likely heading back to shore," Krom said.

"Quiet!" said the Tieren, not fully understanding the conversation. "We talk to leader."

"It will be too late by then!"

"How we know you friend not take box?" said the Tieren.

"Trust us, we don't have it."

"We go; the commander talk to you."

***

Seth had started to doze off when he heard a ferocious knock on the commander's door, broadcast through the implant. The Tieren leader ran to the door, swung it wide open, and stood at the threshold. Seth saw his guards holding two prisoners. "They captured Krom," said Seth.

"That's just great," said Keph. "What are they going to do with them?"

"They haven't decided yet. Furthermore, there's no sign of the Transcript. I'll keep monitoring," said Seth.

Just then, the door opened, causing Keph to turn around. "More bad news sir," said one of the guards. "Maklober escaped from jail last night."

"What!" cried out Keph. "Where is he?"

"We assume he has left the Kitab and is on his way back to Wellen."

"And the Transcript?"

"No idea."

"Lewy, what the hell is going on?" demanded Keph.

"Maklober must have gone after Moch," he said.

"Who is Moch?"

"He is the one who stole the Transcript in the first place. Maklober is a detective in Wellen and came to the Kitab on his own to hunt him down."

"Okay, call your friend Joseph and have the prisoners returned once they arrive in Wellen." Lewy called, but Wellen hadn't seen them yet.

"For now, you and Seth will remain here as my prisoners until this whole thing is sorted out," said Keph.

"Is that really necessary," asked Lewy, speaking on behalf of Seth.

"I just want to simplify matters. I can't have groups of people roaming around the Kitab," said Keph.

"Don't worry, Keph, we won't give you any trouble," said Lewy nervously. Seth looked at both of them sheepishly. After a few minutes, Lewy and Seth went back to the task at hand. Lewy then spoke in a perfunctory tone, "Keph, forget about Maklober. His mission is noble. Once he and Moch return to Wellen, we can work something out between you and Moch. In the meantime, he will be needed to testify against another group, the Directors."

"That is of no concern to the Kitab," Keph said.

Chapter 19

Moch made his way to the entry point at the Port of Lub. He still had the Transcript in hand. To his surprise, he found Maklober's boat and figured that this must have been his route of entry. Moch only knew of this keyhole entrance by air. He untied the boat and slowly paddled away. At the very least, Maklober had to still be in the Kitab. After the rather long and arduous journey, Moch arrived at the intermediate port of Lamin. Typically, tourists are taken via helicopter to the Kitab from this location. He was at a loss at this point. Rather than attempting to sail the rest of the way on this little craft, he stopped at the port and checked into a nearby hotel. At least here, there would be no Mahlpatrol or other sources looking for him; for the moment anyway.

***

Maklober took cover in a warehouse on the dock. He waited and planned out his next move. He didn't know where Moch was, but figured he was either in Tieren custody or on his way back to Wellen. He also didn't know that Krom had been captured. Rather than getting tangled up with the Tieren, he decided to head back to Wellen, as he felt he could do more from that end. He secretly hoped that Moch was on his way to Wellen, either with or without the Transcript. He figured that Lewy must be a hostage by now. *They won't hurt him, though*, he thought. At nightfall, he ran to the entry point, but to his chagrin did not find the boat. He went back to the dock and looked around for any mode of transportation. No one was on the dock per Mahlpatrol's orders. He saw guards making rounds and tried to duck in between the buildings. He then spotted a single, small motorboat anchored to the pier. A guard was standing between him and the boat. There was no one in the near vicinity. His knee was still hurting and shoulder had recovered enough for him to sneak up to the guard. The guard heard him and confronted him. In the dim light of the moon and nearby lamp poles, he made out the familiar uniform of the Kitab.

"Turn around and return to your quarters," said the guard. Maklober continued to advance. Before the guard was able to hold up his rifle to shoot, Maklober lunged into him, head on. The guard let out a cry and then they both fell on the ground. Maklober delivered a succession of quick punches to his face. The man fell silent, but was still breathing. Maklober could hear guards running in the distance, shouting at him to stop. Maklober quickly got up and ran to the boat. This was one of the launches needed to offload small items from the ships. He jumped in, cursing the sputtering motor. Finally, it roared into action. He raced to the entryway amidst shouts and gunfire from the guards. The guards sounded the alarms, but by the time they had run back to their boats, Maklober had disappeared into the night. He then sailed the long journey back but only to the intermediate port of Lamin as Quine was too far. As the Kitabians have no jurisdiction beyond the Port of Lub, they couldn't follow him.

The guards informed Keph of these developments. Keph was furious and now relied on Seth to keep him informed. In his anger, he decided to double the guard in the computer room.

***

Moch checked into a hotel and stayed in his room till evening. He got the penthouse suite, the last one left. Once he was convinced that no one was looking for him, he went down to the hotel restaurant for dinner. The place was a dive but the food was good. Afterwards, he went to the bar where an old washed-up singer was attempting to revive the hits of the past few decades. He ordered a Scotch and sat back at one of the corner tables, out of plain sight. He lit up a cigarette, as cigars were not allowed. As he sat, thinking about the next step, he was suddenly startled by a woman asking if she could share his table as the rest were taken. He thought before he spoke. She was rather attractive and appeared disarming. She had platinum blonde hair with sparkling blue eyes and a hot-looking body; probably in her forties.

"By all means, please sit down," he said rather dryly. "Would you like a smoke?" he asked.

"No thanks. Are you a tourist or one of the locals?" said the woman.

"I'm actually a tourist, but have to change plans and return home. I intended to visit the Kitab, but business calls."

"I can understand that," said the woman. "I am also here on vacation. I just came back from the Kitab. What a mess over there. There was all this commotion. The Mahlpatrol made us all leave. We couldn't even finish our tour."

"What bad luck," said Moch.

"Yeah, I had wanted to visit for quite some time."

"Well, perhaps you could return another time," said Moch.

"Sorry, mister, it ain't worth it," said the woman.

Moch thought perhaps he could join her on the return trip, disguised as friends.

"By the way, what's your name?" asked Moch.

"Oh, sorry, I'm Gena."

"And your name?" she asked.

Moch thought quickly and said, "Chet." He continued, "Are you planning to return tomorrow, or are you staying longer?"

"I'm booked on the morning ship," she said.

"That's my plan too. By the way, are you traveling alone?"

"No, I'm part of a tour group," said Gena.

"Where are they now?"

"Probably up in their rooms; a boring lot. I just went along for security reasons."

"I understand," said Moch.

"So, what line of work are you in, Chet?" asked Gena.

"I'm involved in security at one of the local hotels in Wellen. There has been a rash of thefts requiring my return." Moch looked at her in the dim light of the bar. He hadn't had sex in a while, and was quite attracted to her. He made more small talk. "How about you?" he said.

"I'm an administrator for one of the corporations in town. We deal in stocks."

"Sounds interesting," said Moch. He then said casually, "Hey, how about a nightcap?"

Gena agreed, and they left the bar. She stayed with him all night. The sex was great. The next morning, they got up, showered, and went down to breakfast. She met up with her tour group. After exchanging the usual pleasantries, Moch bought a ticket when Gena slipped away to the rest room. There was no added security. Moch felt safe for now. She returned from the restroom, and they boarded the ship together. The trip was short. Conversation was light. Upon arrival he quickly ran to catch a cab, after wishing goodbye to Gena.

She cried out, "Can we get together some time, Chet?"

He replied quickly and said, "Sure." She scribbled her name on a piece of paper and urged him to call her. He said fine and darted away.

***

Maklober made it to Lamin uneventfully. He called Billy, his lieutenant, to arrange for a helicopter to fly him back. His first stop, however, was Quine to pick up his badge from the sailor and apologize for losing his boat. "We found it," said the sailor. "It was anchored at a dock in Lamin."

Moch was here, Maklober thought. Upon landing in Wellen, he saw Moch leaving the ship in a cab. He told the pilot to radio the lieutenant to follow him. Squad cars encircled the car.

Billy jumped out and said, "Get out slowly, and no tricks."

Maklober joined up with the lieutenant.

"Long time, no see, man!" said Billy.

"It feels like an eternity," said Maklober.

"You're just in time."

As the driver was getting out of the car, Moch snuck out the back. "Oh no you don't," said Maklober. He raced ahead on foot and caught up to him, tackling and then pinning him to the ground. "You're mine now, Moch," said Maklober.

Moch was seething. The uniformed officers arrived. They handcuffed Moch and then read him his rights.

"Hey Maklober," said Billy "that was quite a move. Pick that up from your wrestling days in high school?"

"Yeah, but it was much easier in those days," said Maklober, massaging his shoulder. "By the way, what happened to Chaych?" asked Maklober.

"Oh yeah, I forgot that you have been out of the loop the past several days. Chaych snapped out his trance and won the match. Sci Tech will merge with Libertarian."

"I know that, but how's Chaych?" said Maklober.

"He was undergoing testing the last I heard. I don't know what happened afterwards," said Billy.

"Thanks for the update," said Maklober.

Moch was taken to the precinct. In the interrogation room, Billy and Maklober pumped him for information. He declined to cooperate. "I want my attorney," he said.

"Realistically Moch," said Maklober, "now that the Transcript is back in our hands, the Directors don't need you anymore. They will deny ever knowing you."

"I have a proposition," said the lieutenant. "If you cooperate and are willing to testify against them, I'll ask the district attorney to go easy on you."

"Let me think about it," said Moch.

"Well, don't take too long," said Maklober, "the deal won't be on the table forever."

"Okay, I'll help you. I still want an attorney, though."

Until arrangements could be made, they moved Moch to the city's maximum security prison. The Directors were arrested and held on bond. Attorneys came out of the woodwork in their defense. "As long as we have Moch," said Billy, "all the attorneys in the world won't be able to help them."

"That's a big *if*," said Maklober.

Chapter 20

Maklober and Billy took the Transcript over to the consulate general, and then met Joseph and went over the extraordinary set of circumstances in the Kitab.

"I'm happy to meet you, Maklober. Now that the Transcript is safe, we have some leverage with the Superiors. They are holding Seth and Lewy as hostages."

"Aren't they worried that we will study their software?" said Maklober.

"Don't worry; the contents are meaningless by themselves. We would need the other components to make any sense out of it. Nevertheless, our scientists have made a copy. What I can tell you, though, is that Seth is sending us valuable information obtained from the chip. The Superiors think that only they are witnessing this firsthand, but in actuality, Seth is transmitting it in real time. Furthermore, our linguists are voraciously studying the Tieren language."

"So far, what have you gotten?"

"You know that's classified," said Joseph.

***

Moch was now in jail, awaiting trial. He was entitled to his one telephone call prior to lockup. He was hoping to contact a marker, a warrior, whom he befriended when he was in the Security Council. The warrior was indebted to him from a prior transgression.

Moch knew that he could not call overseas, and instead took a chance. He called on one of their mutual friends in town; luckily the warrior had been visiting for the past month. In the company of policemen, Moch called his friend and spoke in code. As part of the

Security Council's training for their elite members, they were taught to speak in code, which was updated and replaced annually. Luckily, the warrior still remembered Moch's outdated code. After a few minutes of what sounded like casual conversation to those around him, Moch had arranged for an escape the next night. The warrior was familiar with the prison, as his brother had once been held there prior to extradition.

The warrior came in the next morning disguised as an official from the Security Council, demanding that Moch be returned in his custody to be tried in the international court. The warden would not allow this, as Moch was a prisoner, awaiting trial in Wellen.

"I have a proposition," said the warrior. "If you allow us to try him, we will reserve sentencing and punishment."

While the warden pondered this, he suddenly felt the ground move and then heard a deafening explosion in the courtyard. The blast nearly broke his bulletproof window. Furniture had shifted out of position. He ran out and joined the others, who had already gathered in the yard. Some were injured and lying on the ground. The paramedics arrived and were tending to them.

***

Moch steadied himself as the blast shook beneath him. He was then able to escape through an opening in the wall. The warrior had a car waiting. Moch and the warrior met up at their friend's house. Moch was grateful but didn't explain too much. He didn't want them getting involved with his problems. He planned to go underground. He was now a fugitive from both the Kitab and Wellen. He didn't want to endanger his friends further.

***

Maklober was in Billy's office. They were each going over Moch's paperwork when the phone rang. The sound was piercing, breaking their concentration. The lieutenant picked up the phone. After a few seconds, his face turned bright red. Maklober could sense he was about to yell, but restrained himself. "What's wrong?" asked Maklober.

"That was the warden's assistant. That bastard Moch escaped again."

Maklober jumped up from his chair, pounded his fist against the table, and shouted, "What's so tough about keeping this man in jail?" Once the realization and initial shock was over, Maklober said, "This time when I catch him, I'm going to guard him personally."

With that, he ran out into the dark, quiet street in a huff. Maklober knew Moch would go underground, as he had no friends now. The Directors were in custody. They had failed in their attempt to take over control of the Kitab and reinstate their University. *Where to start, though?* he thought. It was personal—his reputation was on the line.

CHAPTER 21

Maklober met up with his assistant to go over paperwork after the Moch fiasco. Once they finished, Maklober reclined in his chair. He folded his arms behind his head and listened as his assistant told him about the Retsel match.

"I left a message on your voicemail after the Retsel match. At the hospital that day, Chaych suddenly sat up in bed, stunned to see the judges, Korbin, and the Retsel board in his room. Nevertheless, he studied the board, and then made the move to capture Korbin's crown. He won the match!" said the assistant.

"I got the message later. I inadvertently turned off my phone in the library," said Maklober.

"Anyway, everyone asked what happened. Chaych said that he had no idea and was completely dumbfounded. Nevertheless, Libertarian University won and remained open. Korbin went over and congratulated Chaych. The judges left and Korbin and I remained."

"Incredible," said Maklober as he lowered his arms to his lap and sat up in the chair shaking his head.

"I know. I wanted to find out more so I asked the doctor what he thought.

"And?"

"The doctor thought he had a warning stroke, a TIA. He was in the process of working up the cause and would know in a couple of days," said the assistant.

"How did Chaych look?" asked Maklober.

"Not too bad. He was lying in the bed with an IV hooked up to his arm. Korbin spoke with him a little about the match and how brilliantly he played. Chaych then suddenly burst out in a rant and got all philosophical. Korbin told him to calm down. Chaych sat up straighter in the bed and furrowed his eyebrows for a few seconds. There was this large vein coursing over his temple and tiny beads of sweat forming over his sideburns. He went to say that in some metaphysical way, what happened to him was similar to the problem in the Kitab. Both had a brief period of mental paralysis. He then lay back down and closed his eyes for a moment before regaining his composure."

"What happened then?" asked Maklober, leaning forward in anticipation.

"He opened his eyes when he heard Korbin and I stand up from our chairs. We asked if he was okay. Without saying a word to each other, Korbin and I instinctively knew that Chaych had not fully recovered. Korbin smiled, patted Chaych on the shoulder and said, 'Get some rest, my friend.' I shook Chaych's hand and walked out with Korbin. We thanked the doctor and left the room. We didn't say anything to each other as we made our way through the hallways and simply parted ways once we reached the entrance to the hospital."

Maklober sat silent for a few seconds, looking pensively toward the ceiling. His assistant began writing some notes. Maklober looked down and began speaking, interrupting the assistant from his work. "In a way, he may have been right."

"How?"

"Well, the Directors wanted to take over the Kitab and the University, thereby paralyzing both the Kitab and preventing Chaych from winning."

"With all due respect, sir, I think you need some rest. It's been a long journey," said the assistant.

"You may be right," said Maklober as he shook his head, laughing.

CHAPTER 22

Nearly two weeks had passed by since the Retsel match. Joseph personally returned the Transcript and apologized profusely to Keph, who reluctantly accepted. The Kitabian scientists inspected the machinery and software and felt that it was still operational. Keph and his aides returned to the central government offices and applied the software to their computer system. All was operational again.

Before leaving, Lewy and Seth asked if they could stay for another month. Keph agreed, but kept them under guard and all information gathered was scrutinized and maintained by the scientists. What he did not know was that Seth was continuously transmitting the information to Wellen.

Krom and his aide were still held in Tieren custody. After painstaking diplomatic efforts, Keph was able to convince the Tieren leader to let them go. Joseph flew back to Wellen. Lewy was relieved and prepared to continue his service with Seth. He was already listed away on sabbatical from his institute.

***

On the day Moch escaped from jail, Billy was holding a previously scheduled press conference detailing the sequence of events from the Retsel match to the present day. He had intended to award Maklober in person with a medal for bravery, but apologized to the crowd, explaining that Maklober was in hot pursuit of Moch. He said a few words about Maklober and his stellar career. He also awarded an honorary ribbon to Lewy in absentia for his heroism. Billy then held up both awards, one in each hand. The audience cheered and the press snapped pictures from the cameras positioned in front of the makeshift stage.

As the ceremonies were about to close, there was a terrific crash at the harbor. The people in the audience turned toward the sound and covered their heads. Some hit the ground and others began running. The lieutenant stared at the harbor, trying to figure out what had happened. Maklober was in hot pursuit—he had received information that Moch had stolen a car and was headed to the airport. At the dock, Moch misjudged the distance between a container and the warehouse and swerved off the road. The car sped into the water. Moments before impact, he was able to jump out. Maklober stopped his car and ran after Moch, who was lying by the dock, barely conscious. Maklober radioed in for an ambulance. Moch was still alive.

"I got you this time," said Maklober.

In a whisper, Moch said, "Keep talking." He gave out a small laugh and lapsed into unconsciousness.

"You just don't give up," said Maklober.

The paramedics arrived and took Moch to the hospital. There were round-the-clock guards in and outside his room. Maklober was about to leave the hospital when Billy came in.

"That was quite a show," he said. "By the way, Maklober, what do you think happened?"

Just as Maklober was about to answer, Yarmin stormed in. "Good luck explaining this one," Billy said.

"Thanks."

Billy quickly excused himself after greeting Yarmin. "By the way, Maklober, I expect to see you first thing in the morning to fill out the paperwork," he said as he left.

"That will be a monumental task," Maklober said.

Maklober was gloating. Yarmin stood there in disgust and quickly brought him back to reality.

"Where the hell were you? I couldn't find you anywhere after the Retsel match," she said.

"I'll fill you in over dinner. I could only leave you a brief message on your answering machine that day," said Maklober. "I'm starving, and this will take a long time."

CHAPTER 23

They drove in silence to their favorite place. When they arrived, the bar was crowded; everyone was glued to the TV screens. Jack, the bartender, spotted them and quickly sat them down at a quiet place in the back, reserved for VIPs. "I thought this would be more appropriate," he said. "We wouldn't want everyone bothering you now that you are a celebrity."

"I appreciate that," said Maklober.

"What can I get you to drink?" said Jack.

"A shot of whiskey for Yarmin, and a beer for me," said Maklober.

They sat looking at the distant TV screens, with the mumble of the newscast hovering over the patrons. Jack returned with the drinks and placed an order for dinner.

"I'm naturally curious, Maklober," said Jack.

"You and the rest of the world," said Maklober.

"What happened over there in the Kitab?" asked Yarmin.

"If you have a few minutes, Jack, I'll explain."

"Just a minute."

Jack had one of his assistants cover the bar. He grabbed a shot of Scotch and sat down at the table. Maklober summarized the events that had transpired thus far. By this time, Yarmin was on her second drink. Dinner had already arrived. Maklober was rapidly trying to eat and explain at the same time his journey through the Kitab. He left out the part about the Tieren.

"That's an interesting story, Maklober. It reminds me of my days in the army," said Jack.

"It was quite an adventure," said Maklober as he took a swig of beer.

"What happened to Chaych? We almost lost to Sci Tech," said Yarmin.

"That's the puzzle. I spoke with my assistant who said that the doctors suspected that Chaych had a transient ischemic attack, a form of a warning stroke. The doctors ran tests to identify the reason," said Maklober.

"I hope he's okay," said Jack.

"Let's keep our fingers crossed," said Maklober.

Jack saw that some customers had come in, got up, and said, "I have to get back to work. Congratulations on catching Moch."

"See you later," they said.

Maklober and Yarmin talked about her latest pursuits; life was back to usual. They went back to Yarmin's place that night. She said, "You're holding back something, Maklober. I know there is more to the story than what you have told us. What happened in the Kitab?"

Maklober was quiet and did not answer.

"I was right," she said.

"Let's drop it for now," said Maklober. "I have to think about this further. There is too much on my mind right now. We captured Moch and intend to keep him locked away until the trial. I have a shitload of paperwork to do tomorrow."

"But you're so tense. I can see it in your eyes," said Yarmin. "I know, you're just trying to unwind." Yarmin massaged his shoulders, but they were rock solid. "It's okay if you want to vent a little. I think you'll feel better." Maklober clenched his fists and pounded them on the table several times. "Feel better?"

He relaxed and sat back in the chair. "A bit, but it will take more than that, I'm afraid."

Yarmin sat next to him and said softly, "I know, but I think the best thing now is some sleep. Let's go to bed." Maklober slowly stood up. He had bags under his eyes from the fatigue. They retired to bed. Yarmin held him tight till he fell fast asleep.

***

"So what really happened in the Kitab?" asked Billy the next morning at headquarters.

"Not you too," said Maklober.

"Yeah, I want to know the real scoop," he said.

"Right now, I'm not sure." As Maklober was about to get up to leave, the phone rang. Billy told Maklober to wait and answered the call. He stayed on the phone longer this time, listening without uttering a word. Maklober intently studied his facial expressions to gauge the nature of the call. He could see the same reaction as last time. Billy's face turned bright red as he hung up the phone. "I'm worried about you, boss. What's going on?" Billy sat back down, rubbing his tired eyes with his hands.

He then looked up at Maklober and said, "That was the hospital."

Maklober could feel his heart sink to his feet. "Uh oh. What happened?"

"It's Moch. There is someone else in his hospital room and he's nowhere to be found!" said Billy, staring straight ahead as he spoke. Maklober stood, perplexed, trying to make sense of what he just heard.

"How did that happen?" he finally said weakly, with a strain in his voice. "Are they sure? How did Moch escape?" He had a million questions running through his head, trying to figure out how this could have happened. "There were guards posted in and outside his room the whole time," said Maklober.

"I know, but apparently when the doctor came in to check in him, he went in alone. He gave instructions to our men not to come in due to privacy reasons," Billy said. "They were given strict instructions to accompany anyone who entered the room. Somehow, this doctor told them it would only take a minute."

Maklober was breathing heavily in anticipation. "So then what happened?"

"Suddenly, there was a lot of panic at the nurse's station. The guards could hear them say that there was a code blue on the floor. Within seconds, they could see a team of doctors and nurses approaching with a crash cart. They burst into Moch's room."

Maklober stood up with sweat streaming down his face. "Then what?"

Billy answered as if he were reading a script, "The details are unclear, but in the chaos, the doctor left the room. When the men went in, the code blue team showed them what they found. The doctor was tied up with IV tubing and gauze was stuffed in his mouth. He was out for the count."

Maklober shook his head and said, "Incredible."

Billy went on, "Yeah, so once they awakened him, he told them he remembered telling Moch that he wanted to examine him, and then that was it. I can only surmise that Moch escaped in the doctor's uniform."

Maklober lifted his eyebrows and curled his upper lip then said, "But no one recognized him?"

Billy replied, "In all that chaos, apparently not. The men went running out to find Moch, but he was gone."

Maklober shook his head and could only say, "Unbelievable." He sat back down and tried to collect himself.

***

By now, reporters were hovering around police headquarters for any information. Billy held a press conference and assured them that they would be the first to know anything. Of course, no one knew about Seth and his project. No one would probably ever know. There was a lot of work to be done now that the universities merged. For the lay public, life returned to normal.

***

Moch ran into the shopping center from the parking lot and bought two changes of clothes with whatever money was in the doctor's wallet. He couldn't withdraw the ten thousand dollar deposit the Directors had given him for his efforts, for he would have surely been caught. He was now wearing a golf shirt with slacks and leather shoes. He bought some hair dye and went into the restroom to alter his appearance. He ditched the doctor's clothes in one of the trash receptacles, then exited. He went outside, cautiously looking out for the police. In front of the mall he saw a police cruiser inching its way across the driveway. He turned back and went inside till they passed. He once again took a chance and saw that the coast was clear. He made his way to the street and quickly hailed a cab.

Moch headed to the outskirts of the city where the road ended and the bush began. He got out and thanked the driver. The cabbie looked at him and said, "Are you crazy, mister? This is the bush, a dangerous place, I hear."

Moch winked at the driver and flashed a smile. "Oh, don't worry, I know what I'm doing," he said. The cabbie waited for a few minutes, shook his head, then turned around and drove back to the city. When Moch could no longer see the car, he changed into a long sleeved shirt, khaki pants, and sturdy hiking shoes. He ditched the shopping bag in the brush, then took a leak. He zipped up his fly and turned to enter the densely-vegetated path to the southern port of the island. He was now a fugitive of Wellen, the Kitab, and the Tieren society.

As he was contemplating his predicament, he caught an image from the corner of his eye and suddenly froze. "Welcome to the bush," said Maklober, grinning and holding a pair of shiny new handcuffs glistening under the sun's brilliant rays. Moch shook his head, then darted to the right and tried to make a run for it; but this time Maklober lunged forward and tackled him to the hard, sun-dried ground. He grabbed Moch's arms and snapped on the handcuffs. "Gotcha."